# TOTO
# & the Cats of
# OZ

## By
## Robin Hess

### Illustrated by
### Andrew Hess

# To My Wonderful Children:

*It was their demands for more Oz books (after I had read them all there were) that pushed me into my first attempt to write a book - this book. I am eternally grateful to them, not just for that insistence, but for the great adults they have become.*

Robin Hess's *Christmas in Oz* is available from Amazon.com or Books of Wonder (16 West 18th St, New York, New York 10011, www.booksofwonder.com)

Robin Hess's *L. Frank Baum and the Perfect Murder* is available from Amazon.com

Ozmapolitan Press/FIRST EDITION, November 5, 2013
Published in the United States of America by Ozmapolitan Press.
Distributed through Amazon.com.

The ornamental initials at the beginning of each chapter were designed by Bill Eubank for the International Wizard of Oz Club, Inc. (www.ozclub.org), and are used by permission of the Club.

Self-cataloging Data
Hess, Robin 1927--  .
        Toto and the cats of Oz / Hess, Robin
ISBN -1453836527
Originally published: [Vashon, WA] : [Ozmapolitan Press].
        I. Title  II. Fairy Stories. III. Oz.
813.08766

Printed in United States of America
10 9 8 7 6 5 4 3 2 1

# A Note to My Readers

October 28, 2013

What a marvelous invention is the cell phone. In the old days all you could do with your home telephone was to connect into the telephone line that went by your home. Now with a cell phone, you can connect to any sender anywhere.

Thus it was that the other day, when my cell phone rang, I was caught off guard when I heard a young lady's voice say, "Hello, Robin, this is Dorothy." I paused as I tried to think of what Dorothy I knew who might be calling me. In the pause, she said, "You know, Dorothy Gale in the Emerald City."

Well, you can believe I was flabbergasted.

She told me there have been some things going on in Oz that that ought to be reported to the outside world and since I was interested in doing such reporting, she and the others thought I should know about them. It took about twenty calls over the next couple weeks before she could complete the story, but now it can be told and here it is.

Happy reading to each and every one of you. Let me know how you like this and whether I should keep on reporting. Dorothy said there are a number of other events that need to be known, too.

My love to each of you,
Robin Hess
27727 94th Ave. SW
Vashon WA 98070
hesses2go@hotmail.com

# Table of Contents

# Chapter 1

# Ozma Calls a Council

h Toto, Toto. Where are you? Here, Toto. Here, Toto!" The words echoed back across the empty Ballroom as Dorothy dropped down on a bench by one of the great windows.

Where else could she look now? Pulling at the edge of the pretty white pinafore that covered her gingham dress, she tried to think. Suddenly a commotion at the far end of the room interrupted her thoughts. The door popped open and in tumbled a cascade of color. Turning toward it, Dorothy called out, "Scraps! What on earth?"

Completing a turn, a twist and a cartwheel, the Patchwork Girl came to rest and explained, "The door stuck — I think. I heard you calling and wondered what was going on."

"I can't find Toto," said Dorothy. "I have looked all over the place and in the gardens and just everywhere, but I still don't find him. I started as soon as I got back to my room after breakfast, and here I am, still looking. I can't think where to try next."

1

# Toto and the Cats of Oz

"You have lost your dog?
How can it be?
Look behind a log,
Check it out quickly.

If he's not around,
Ask our good fairy.
He's sure to be found,
Indubitably."

Reciting as she twirled on her toes, the Patchwork Girl gave a last fast spin on the final word and came to rest again. She scratched at the yellow yarn that served for hair upon her head, looked quizzically at Dorothy

*The Patchwork Girl gave a last fast spin . . .*

# Ozma Calls a Council

and finally said, "Well, what about it? Have you asked Ozma?"

With a look of surprise, Dorothy jumped up and started dragging Scraps toward the main door. "Why no! How silly of me. I just kept thinking he would be around the next corner, but he never was."

Rushing through the halls of the most beautiful palace you can imagine, and right in the middle of the wondrous Emerald City of Oz, Dorothy and Scraps ignored it all as they tried to recall where they had last seen Toto.

"I remember seeing him yesterday," said Scraps. "It was when you were eating breakfast and he was eating with those other cats."

"Yes, I remember that," replied Dorothy. "He was seated between that huge new cat, Alexander, and that horrid scroungy black cat, Joom. Toto has spent too much time with them during the past couple days, and I don't like it. There's something creepy about that black one."

"I know what you mean. I've never seen a cat quite like that before. Don't like the feel of it at all."

"Oh, Scraps, I'm so worried. He has not been to a meal since yesterday morning—a day-and-a-half! I should have done something when he did not come in to sleep last night, but I just figured he'd be waiting at the door this morning. Oh, what could have happened to poor Toto?"

Doing a comical pirouette around the last corner, the Patchwork Girl tried to sound lighthearted as she answered, "Don't worry. He's probably out chasing butterflies."

Little comforted, and with her worry still showing in her face, Dorothy looked right and left, panting a little as they hastened to the chambers of the ruling princess of Oz. There they met Jellia Jamb, Ozma's pretty little maid-in-waiting. As soon as Dorothy explained her problem, Jellia began hurrying them through the Palace.

"Ozma just went down to the Great Garden," the green-clad girl explained. "She thought she heard you calling out there a bit ago."

"She probably did," replied Dorothy. "I have been everywhere trying to find Toto."

Talking as they ran, all three dashed down the stairs and out into the Garden. Dorothy and Jellia successfully managed two steps at a time, but Scraps, trying for three, was soon rolling down the stairs like a colorful ball of cotton. This is of course, just what she is anyway — a giant patchwork doll, sewn together and stuffed with cotton. She was brought to life with some magic Powder of Life concocted by Dr. Pipt. Although she lives and talks and laughs and makes up ridiculous poetry, her cotton stuffings never get hurt when she falls, and her cotton body never gets hungry or tired.

At the bottom of the stairs she unrolled and sprawled out as she slid across the floor. Almost immediately she was back on her feet, still five steps ahead of the other two, who, at any other time would have been nearly helpless with laughter. But, so intent were they on their mission, they hardly noticed the incidental antics of their

# Ozma Calls a Council

companion.

Bursting through the outside doors, they came upon such a scene as would make any mortal stand still in amazement. However, so long had they been in the Emerald City that, in their anxiety, they rushed through the familiar beauty of Ozma's Great Garden as though it wasn't even there. No more breathtaking garden has ever been seen. So carefully and artfully was it designed that it gave the impression of stretching for endless miles, yet it was all contained in a mere seven acres.

There, on the far side of the Garden, was it a purple mountain or was it a luxurious growth of wisteria? Here, near by, a brook meandered through emerald green banks as the sun glistened like gold on the tip of each little wavelet, or was it a long, winding bed of glowing pansies? And those dogs down there, were they really chasing a poor fox they were about to close in upon, or were they closely and carefully trimmed boxwood bushes? New scenes greeted the eye as the path wound through ever more surprising and beautiful designs in flowers.

Here there were no magical plants, but only the everyday, ordinary bushes and flowers that might be found almost anywhere in the world. It was only the mortal skills of the master gardeners that arranged all this so as to mystify and delight the beholder.

Each of the searchers went a different direction. Dorothy headed for a spot where flowers and bushes were fashioned into a nearly impenetrable jungle, with only a few twisting and winding paths. Running along the fuchsia-lined North Path, she called, "Ozma, are you here? Ozma-a-a!"

Off to her right she heard an answering, "Dorothy, is that you?"

"Here. Yes. Oh Ozma! It's dreadful! Toto has been stolen! Ozma-a-a! Where are you?"

Turning down narrow side paths and more trails, the two girls kept calling back and forth, using their voices to guide one another. Finally, pushing a branch back out of the path she was on, Dorothy saw Ozma coming around a bend in front of her.

"Oh Ozma," she burst out, "how can we get Toto back?"

Not every girl would speak with such lack of ceremony to a powerful ruler such as the Princess Ozma, but Dorothy has been her best friend for many, many years. Imagine that! A poor little girl from a poor little farm in Kansas, moving into a great palace, being made a princess, and becoming the close companion of the lovely young Queen of Oz. This is not just any queen, but a fairy queen, ruler of the largest and best known fairyland there is anywhere at all. Powerful in her own magical arts, she has the additional support of the talents of the world's greatest magic workers—the resourceful little Wizard of Oz, and Glinda the Good Witch, ruler of the Quadling Country, the southern part of Oz. Glinda had supported her from the beginning. The Wizard, who had been a humbug and left Oz in a balloon, later returned and learned real magic from Glinda so he could live in the Emerald City as an advisor to Ozma.

# Ozma Calls a Council

The sweet girl that is Queen of all Oz has not been spoiled by all this power. She still lets no formalities stand between her and her friends. And here she was, wearing a pair of rather faded jeans, once white tennis shoes that were now no particular color at all, and an old green blouse with rolled up sleeves. When she first heard Dorothy's anxious calls she had turned quickly to see what she could do to help. Now, as she took Dorothy's hands in her own, she said, "Toto? What has happened?"

Incoherency tumbled from Dorothy's mouth: "Havent seetoto yewsterday bkfast. He didnshoup lasnight, sumed hewus ousidedoing hisownthng dintshow breakfat, anddn eatbitmself thmorning."

"Whoa!" laughed Ozma. "You've left me way behind. Slow down a little and maybe you can say that a little more clearly."

Giggling a bit, Dorothy tried again. Speaking more slowly and thinking of what she was saying, she was able to tell Ozma as much as she knew.

Hesitating a little, Ozma asked, "Do you think that strange cat, Joom, could have had something to do with it?"

"Ooh," shivered Dorothy. "That's exactly what I'm afraid of - that creepy cat. But then he hasn't been around for a few days."

"All the more reason it might be him," replied Ozma. "I think I had better call the Council together! We'll find Toto for you." But her voice lacked confidence.

# Chapter 2

# In The Throne Room

s the two old friends ran back through the garden together, they called out for Scraps and Jellia to join them. By the time they had reached the Great Gates of the Garden, both of these other two had appeared, coming down other paths.

Ozma started giving instructions as soon as they came in sight: "Scraps would you run right up to the tower to ring the bells for an emergency meeting of the Council? Jellia, dear, I think maybe you could go through the palace asking everyone you meet if they've seen Toto. And it would be best for you, Dorothy, to go straight to the Throne Room. Maybe you can fill in some details for early arrivals. I want to have time to talk to the Wizard a little about this before we all meet."

With these words, each of the girls sped upon her own special mission.

Soon Dorothy was standing on the regal balcony of the Throne Room, looking over the great Emerald City and gazing upon one of the typically beautiful Ozian sunsets. It glowed upon a hundred towers in the city, their gleaming greenness muted by the touch of the

# In The Throne Room

twilight's rosy hues. Though the sweep of soft colors and the glitter of the sparkling jeweled towers would have held her attention on any other evening, at this time Dorothy had room in her thoughts only for her missing little black dog.

Indeed, so preoccupied was she that she did not notice the approach of footsteps until the softly gruff voice of her Uncle Henry announced his presence.

"What's this, honey? Is Toto really stolen?"

With a startled jerk, she turned toward him, "Oh Uncle Henry! What can I do? I'm afraid Toto is in some real danger!" Running to him, she buried her head in his faded blue coveralls and started to cry.

Although he was one of the important people in the Queen's Council, Uncle Henry seldom dressed in anything other than old denim. In the evenings and for special occasions he liked dressing in fine clothes just like any of the other men of the court. However, during the day, puttering around in the gardens of the palace, both floral and vegetable, and working on repairs and other odd jobs, it would not do to be dressed in fancy clothes. Besides, after sixty-five years of life on a Kansas farm, working hard in clothes like these, it just seemed the natural way to him. Now he had spent twice that long in Oz, but the old ways, clothing and habits still came easiest to him and his wife, Aunt Em.

After a cyclone had carried off their home, things just went from bad to worse. Their farm was being taken by the bank. Aunt Em and Uncle Henry would go to the County Home, Dorothy out to work for a living at the tender age of eleven, and what would become of Toto? It was then that Ozma intervened, over one hundred years ago, to bring them all to Oz.

Now Uncle Henry and Aunt Em could have anything they wished for, but they chose to live in a little, white frame house much like their old one back on the Kansas prairie — only this one was always freshly painted, with an abundance of beautiful flowers around it and every convenience they really wanted in it. Although they did not have to do any work now, both Uncle Henry and Auntie Em still preferred keeping busy doing useful things. Mostly this meant a little farming out back of their cottage, working in the palace gardens, repairing anything Henry put his mind to or cooking and sewing of all sorts by Em.

Placing his strong arm around his little niece's shoulder, the old farmer said, "That's OK girl. You just have yourself a good cry. Everyone's worried, but no one as much as you are." Then as more tears began to fall upon the crisp whiteness of her pinafore, he continued, "Toto's your dog, and you've a right to a good bucket of tears right now."

With that, Dorothy's sobs broke into full force. For several minutes she clung to her Uncle Henry. After a while she pulled a handkerchief from her pocket and daubed at the corners of her eyes, saying, "There! That feels better, but I'm still worried!"

"And well you should be until he comes back," responded her Uncle.

Turning back to the view out over the city, she could

# In The Throne Room

see that the colors were darkening, and flickering dots of light were beginning to blink on here and there in the homes and shops and parks of the capital city.

"Look out there," she said. "Isn't that peaceful and wonderful? And the ringing of the bells, so beautiful. Just listen! Who would think that there was anything wrong in our lovely Emerald City?"

What a shock it would have been for Dorothy if she had known how much trouble that city would soon have, but she continued her reverie: "See, way over in the east is the crown of the gate where Toto and I first came in to see the Wizard. That was back when he was a 'humbug.' He did not know anything about real wizarding then. It was in this very room that he met us — the Cowardly Lion, the Scarecrow the Tin Woodman, and Toto and me. It was Toto who unmasked him. He had fooled us with some old stage tricks and we did not know any better until Toto accidentally knocked down the screen that hid him. Then he was revealed to us, all unaware we were watching him pulling strings, pushing levers and speaking into megaphones. I guess he felt rather foolish when he saw us, but then, having been tricked in that way made us feel foolish too.

"Oh Uncle Henry, Toto simply has to be safe someplace!"

As they talked on the balcony, others began to gather in the Throne Room. The first of these was the Shaggy Man. At one time, before coming to Oz, he had been a penniless wanderer, dressed in tattered rags. That is how he had come to be known as the Shaggy Man in the

# Toto and the Cats of Oz

first place. Now, as one of Dorothy's closest friends and an advisor to Queen Ozma, he was no longer penniless, although money really has little meaning in Oz. Now he dressed in silks and satins, but they were always cut with beautiful tatters — the most elegant rags in town. And, he was still a wanderer — having traveled to practically every corner of the Land of Oz as well as to most of her neighbors across the burning yellow sands of the Deadly Desert.

No sooner had he entered by one door than a clatter was heard in the outer hall. At the far end of the great room another door opened and in pranced one of the most amazing beasts you have ever seen, accompanied by a feverish young man half in and half out of a suit of shining armor.

"Odds bodkins!" he exclaimed as he struggled at strapping a great sword around the waist of his metal breeches. "What's going on here, M'lass? If anyone has harmed a hair of Toto's head I shall run the blighter through. He has Sir Hokus of Pokes to deal with now!" So saying, he dropped the remainder of his armor and ran across the room toward Dorothy.

Knowing what would come next, she was already untying a blue ribbon from her hair by the time he reached her. Once there, he clanked down upon one knee and cried, "A boon, a boon, grant me a boon and I will defend you and fight for your honor and look far and wide 'til Toto is found."

"Here is your boon, my knight," giggled Dorothy as she handed him her ribbon. She was quite accustomed to

# In The Throne Room

his Medieval ways, having rescued him from stagnation in the slow-moving land of Pokes many years earlier. Even so, his old-world habits always amused her and now brought laughter to her lips in spite of her distress over Toto's disappearance.

"Hear my pledge," cried the knight. "I shall not sleep in my own bed, nor eat at my own table 'til Toto is found!"

Taking his hand to signal him to rise, Dorothy gave him a kiss on the forehead before she turned to pat the head of the curious creature who had entered the room with him.

Well known in the Land of Oz, and one of the first of Ozma's companions, he was made completely of wood and looked something like a small horse. Indeed, before life, he had been a carpenter's wooden sawhorse made of a five foot long small tree with four more straight sticks for support. Ozma had found him and brought him to life, adding twigs for ears and a tail. Now he was the fastest and most stalwart steed in all the land. However, he was rather uncomfortable to ride, for, just like a regular carpenter's sawhorse he did not have a middle joint in his legs. This gave him a strange, stiff-legged way of running that could joggle a rider quite a bit. To solve this problem, people usually rode in a beautiful red carriage Ozma had had built especially for him to pull. Even with it full of people, he could still travel faster than the wind.

Now another man encased in metal clanked in through one of the other doors. However, this one moved with jerky, automatic motions, for there was no flesh or blood inside his round, copper casing. He was the famous mechanical man, known as Tik-Tok and created by Smith and Tinker for the King of Ev. He had been hidden in a cave, but discovered by Dorothy on her second trip to Oz.

His steps were getting slower as he came through the door, and with a slow whirring sound he said, "Hur-ry! Some-one wind me up. I came as quick-k-k---." With his mouth wide open, he took six more steps, each moving more slowly, and then stopped dead in mid-stride.

"Land sakes, and I had almost caught up with him," declared a sprightly little old lady who came through the door behind him. "Here, let me take care of you. I don't know what you men would do without us women to look after you!"

With experienced hands she started winding. First she took the key from its secure peg on his back. Then she found the key hole under his left arm where she could wind his thinking mechanism. Almost immediately there was the sound of whirring machinery. She then located a second key hole under his right arm, and even before she had finished winding, he started speaking.

"Oh, thank you, Aunt Em! I guess I have just been do-ing too much to-day and got run down. An-y-way, I head-ed right here as soon as I heard the bells ring out their call for our Coun-cil. What is the prob-lem?"

"Here now," said Aunt Em, "your talking machinery is going to run down as fast as I wind it up if you don't stop a-jabberin' so much. I know no more than you right now, but I s'pose we will all know more as soon as Ozma

# In The Throne Room

gets here."

Aunt Em always talked rapidly and she usually had a lot to say, but everyone seemed to understand and figured that this was her right. After all, she had worked a long lifetime, side by side with Uncle Henry.

Finishing with the second winding spot, she turned now to the third one, located in the middle of the copper man's back. With this winding complete, he would be enabled to move his arms and legs. Standing quite still until she had finished her work, he then bowed as well as he could, touched his hand to his copper hat, and again said, "Thank you, dear Aunt Em."

By this time two great beasts crouched, one on either side of the big throne. On the left, trying not to show his trembling, was a large, tawny lion with a heavy mane. Each time a door opened he would look nervously in that direction. Even a stranger would know that this was the famous Cowardly Lion of Oz, but not so evident was the fact that behind those nervous actions beat one of the bravest, most loyal hearts in the land.

On the other side of the throne sat another great feline. He also looked quickly toward each new movement at the doors, but as he slowly moved his tongue across his lower lip, it was plain that his concern was not one of fear, for this beautiful animal was none other than the Hungry Tiger of Oz. Although his gleaming white teeth could have quickly made a meal of any of the flesh and blood people in the room, his conscience always kept him from doing what his stomach suggested. Indeed, even though he growled a lot about being hungry, he

# Toto and the Cats of Oz

seldom really was, for Ozma saw to it that he was well fed. Even if his stomach were empty, he never really looked with appetite upon anyone. Like most of us, he was more bluff than bite.

As the two large cats sat, looking from side to side and flicking their tails now and then, there entered a tall, thin soldier, dressed from head to toe in a green uniform — that of a Captain General of Oz. In truth, he was the entire Army of Oz. Over his shoulder he carried a long and rather decrepit looking musket with a fresh bouquet of flowers in its muzzle. From his chin flowed the most unbelievable whiskers you have ever seen. Not only did they go all the way down to his knees, but they were a shining natural green! Only in the Land of Oz could such a thing happen.

Walking to the foot of the throne, and ignoring the two great cats, he carefully lowered his gun from his shoulder in order to check it out. Then, content that there was no ammunition in it, on it, or near it, he pounded it five times, and with considerable force upon the bottom step of the throne. This great royal seat was made of solid gold, covered with enough precious jewels to purchase an ordinary kingdom. These glittered and glowed almost as if they were filled with an internal light of their own.

As Omby Amby, for that is the name of the Soldier with the Green Whiskers, struck the steps, a sound echoed from them and throughout the hall like the tones of a deep-throated bell. Alternating with those rolling notes, he called out, "Way! Make way for the Queen! Make way for the Queen! Way!"

# In The Throne Room

With the last stroke upon the step, the doors to the left of the throne burst open and in stepped the lovely young Queen holding lightly to the left arm of the Wizard of Oz. She had not had time to change clothes since she met Dorothy out in the garden, only to slip a clean and colorful green smock over them. Behind them came Scraps and Jellia Jamb, each carrying a very distinctive cat.

Scrap's had in her arms one named Eureka that seemed ordinary enough at first, that is, until a moment after entering the room its soft white fur turned to a muted green. One might think she reflected the dominant green of the curtains and furniture of that beautiful room. But during the course of the Council meeting she would probably change colors a couple more times. No one knew how she came by this most unusual talent. When Dorothy found her in America, she was just a plain white cat, so what was her surprise to discover that, in the Land of Oz, her kitten could magically change the color of her fur.

As for the cat in Jellia's arms, she had no color at all, for she was made of the purest, crystal clear glass. Although Bungle, the Glass Cat, and Scraps were the oldest of friends, she would never let Scraps pick her up for fear the exuberant Patchwork Girl might stumble and drop her. Indeed, she and Scraps had both come to life in the workshop of old Dr. Pipt, the Crooked Magician, years and years ago.

Just as the Princess took her place on the throne, another commotion arose at the far end of the hall. The door opened and streaks of light flashed through it into the room. Then a most peculiar looking beast trotted in followed by two more little girls about Dorothy's age and an old sailor, hobbling along on one wooden peg leg.

The three people, Trot, Betsy Bobbin and Cap'n Bill, were regular people like Dorothy. Many years before, on their own adventures, they had come from the world of America to this wondrous fairyland of Oz. Except for Cap'n Bill's wooden leg, these three were ordinary enough looking, but I imagine that almost anyone would stop to stare at the strange animal that had come into the Throne room with them. He was one of a kind — a Woozy. Unlike all other animals, he had no round places on him. Every part of him was squared off, like leather boxes: a big one for the body, four more, long, thin ones for legs, and a square one for a head with a hinged bottom for his lower jaw. He had no hair except for three little tufts at the tip of his tail. The flashes of light were coming from his eyes, an occurrence that happened whenever he was upset. Altogether, he made a truly amazing sight. He, too, had been an early friend of the Patchwork Girl.

Although they did not know it yet, all those who had gathered in the Great Throne Room would soon be participating in one of the most unexpected adventures of all, with yet more of their friends being drawn into this near disaster.

# Chapter 3

## Where Is Toto?

hat's this?" the Woozy was demanding. "I hear Toto has been dog-napped!" With each word, flashes of light darted from his angry eyes.

Turning cartwheels toward him, the Patchwork Girl responded:

"Ho, now let's not get excited!
No one knows just what has happened,
Know not where he has been taken.
All we know is: we're not knowin'."

The last words and the last cartwheel brought her right in front of the Woozy where she leaned over and patted him on the head.

"Is that what this is all a-bout?" asked Tik-Tok.

"Yes," declared Ozma. "Perhaps Dorothy should tell us what has happened.

Dorothy carefully explained her problem. At the conclusion, Princess Ozma added, "This may relate to those vagabond cats."

"Joom and Alexander!"

"I'll bet they did it."

"Wouldn't s'prise me at all if that Joom were a magician!" declared Aunt Em.

"Never did like those two!" exclaimed the Glass Cat.

"Oh, you don't like any real cats!" countered Trot.

With a little giggle of agreement, Eureka gave a flick of her tail and a wink of her eye as she said, "That's true. She thinks glass is just so superior to flesh." Then, more seriously, she added, "This time, though, I really have to agree with her. I don't like Joom either."

At that, Bungle sniffed, as she rather stiffly and slowly walked across the room, every bit the picture of a cat with a superiority complex, exactly as Eureka had just been describing her.

Pausing to watch her glass friend's deliberate steps, the little cat finally resumed, "No, Joom just does not act like a sensible cat, but now Alexander, he's not half bad if he would just stay away from that dumb black cat."

Their difference of a few minutes before forgotten, Bungle agreed, "As a matter of fact he's not like any cat I've ever met before."

"Yes, Joom does seem a little strange," said the Woozy.

"That's right," added Aunt Em. "Several times I have seen him stroll past our bird bath, paying no attention at all to the birds in it."

"So you sup-pose those two took To-to?" queried Tik-Tok.

"It could be possible," answered the Queen. "I might as well tell you all now. I, too, have my doubts about that Joom, and just before starting this meeting the Wizard

# Where Is Toto?

and I had a little talk."

As she turned to him, the chubby little Wizard began, "We think Joom may not be what he seems — just a vagabond cat, with a lot of good stories. What we believe is that he is some sort of magician!" After the "Oh's" and "Ah's" had subsided, and Aunt Em had muttered, "I told you so!" he continued. "There is something about him that seems strange to each of us."

"He gives me a really eerie feeling," added the little royal Princess. "I don't like it a bit!"

"But," remarked the Shaggy Man, "if he is a magician, why did he spend so much time in the Emerald City during the last few weeks?"

"Yes," said Uncle Henry, "if he'd not meant any trouble, he would've said who he really was, and if he did mean trouble, you'd think he would've gotten started on it sooner than this."

"Well, that is just possible," replied Ozma. "He may have started trouble we do not know about yet."

"Land-a-mercy, not to mention the trouble we already know?" questioned Aunt Em.

"Odds bodkins! None of this is helping us find Toto!" declared Sir Hokus. "A damsel's in distress and naught hath been done to right the wrong. Forsooth, I'd gladly slay a dragon to free Toto, but where is he?"

"What do you mean, 'Where is he?'" spoke a small voice from the door nearest Sir Hokus. "I just got here. Did something happen to Toto?" It was Button-Bright. A great favorite with everyone, he was, indeed, like a bright little button — always getting lost and always turning up when least expected. Originally he had lived in Philadelphia, but he had popped up so often in Oz that this was now considered his home.

Trot, a friend of his in many adventures, ran over to him, saying, "It's dreadful! Toto has been stolen and no one knows where to find him."

"Tarnation!" exclaimed Uncle Henry, "Here we sit talkin', when all we gotta do is go up an' look in that Magic Picture! I don't know why all us smart people never thought o' that 'afore!"

Everyone responded in a general murmur of approval, above which could be heard the clicking of Tik-Tok's voice: "That should set-tle the prob-lem pret-ty quick-ly."

"Yes, and you may all come with me right now. Wherever he is, I guess we all want to know what has happened," said the lovely little Queen.

With that she rose from her throne, took Dorothy by the hand and led the whole Council up to her apartment. Once there, they all went directly to the magnificent green drapery covering the east wall of the room. Jellia Jamb pulled the cord, revealing one of the greatest treasures of Oz — the Magic Picture! To look at it, you might think it was just like any other picture on the wall of any big office in America — until you watched for a bit. For, as you watched, the scene would change. The beautiful meadow just outside the City gates that had been there when Jellia opened the curtains had already been replaced by a view of the Nonestic Ocean with seagulls wheeling in the wind, and now the wooded slopes of the Munchkin Mountains showed. Next might

# Where Is Toto?

be a farmyard scene or a woodland vista or almost anything. Here in this Magic Picture was the ultimate television set, for it would show a person any scene one might choose.

All the gathered Ozians stood now, before this, one of Ozma's oldest pieces of magic equipment. This wonderous picture had helped her solve many different mysteries. Now, the loss of Toto would soon be solved.

Standing thus, viewing the Hammerhead Mountains a little north of Glinda's palace, the Council watched anxiously as Ozma requested, "Please, show us Toto."

The picture blurred in a most unusual way, and everyone gasped at its strange behavior. Nothing recognizable appeared. Instead, the picture became a series of zigzagging lines. Then there were some bright spots and flashes of lights, and the rugged hills of the Hammerhead Mountains reappeared.

"I've never seen that happen before," said the Wizard.

"Nor have I," said Ozma, "not in all the time I have had it."

"Oh me, oh my! What has happened?" moaned the Soldier with the Green Whiskers.

"How will we e-ver find To-to?" worried Tik-Tok.

The always talkative Patchwork Girl was suddenly speechless. All of her usual excitement seemed to have been drained from her.

It was nearly a minute with everyone just standing, helplessly staring, before the Cowardly Lion asked, "Do you suppose we dare try it again?"

"Maybe it did not understand," meowed Eureka.

# Toto and the Cats of Oz

*The picture became a series of zigzagging lines.*

"All right. I will try one more time." Then slowly and clearly, while a peaceful scene along the Munchkin River was showing, Ozma said, "Let me see Toto."

Again the picture blurred, zigzagged, sparked and returned to the beautiful Munchkin River.

"I do not know what to make of it," declared Ozma.

"Should we try asking to see someone else?" asked the Shaggy Man. "What about Jack Pumpkinhead?" asked the Sawhorse.

"Good idea," replied the little Queen, "but first I had better try someone that is quite close. Maybe the picture has been strained a bit. Let me see the Guardian of the Gate."

24

# Where Is Toto?

Immediately and smoothly the scene changed to a little green room with a fat little man in green buckled boots, green breeches, a long green jacket over a frilly green shirt, green eye glasses and a tall green hat. He was playing a game of checkers all by himself.

"I can see that he needs me," chuckled Omby Amby, "but he will just have to go ahead by himself for a while longer."

"And if this does not work, that might be quite a while," said the Woozy.

"Now, let us all be very quiet. I'll try for Jack this time," and turning again to the picture, Ozma spoke slowly, "Show me Jack Pumpkinhead."

Instantly, without a waver, the picture changed to a field of pumpkins. At first a stranger would have thought there was nothing more — just pumpkins. But one stood above the others, and Ozma and all those with her immediately recognized it as a head, stuck on the spindly, clothes-draped wooden body of her oldest friend, the comical man with a carved pumpkin for a head.

Ozma had made him when she was a prisoner of the old Wicked Witch, Mombi, and not even aware of her heritage as the rightful ruler of Oz. Jack was originally dressed in old, cast-off clothing, but now he always wore relatively new clothing. He used to worry about what would happen to him when his pumpkin head grew old and began to spoil, but now he had this whole field of pumpkins. So, any time he thought his head was even a shade too old, he could always carve a new one out of one of his lovely, big new spheres of orange.

# Toto and the Cats of Oz

All those in Ozma's room watched while Jack continued to stroll through his field. Then he stopped and stood awhile, looking all around with a bit of a puzzled look upon his face. Next he began running this way and that, waving his arms wildly as though he was trying to chase something away. And all the time, not another thing was visible but Jack and his pumpkins in their field.

Suddenly, while they watched, all the pumpkins disappeared. It was just like a picture full of lights blinking out, one after another, or a dozen after another, in rapid succession.

Everyone just stood, staring dumbfounded, until

*He began running this way and that, waving his arms*

# Where Is Toto?

Ozma said, "No, no, no! Something is dreadfully wrong. I must look into this."

Then a great clamor arose as everyone began talking at once, all trying to explain what was wrong with the Magic Picture. Each had something to say, but no one could hear what anyone else was saying. Many of them thought that Jack must have learned to do some magic, but no one knew. There was so much noise that finally, at a sign from Ozma, the Soldier with the Green Whiskers rapped the stock of his gun on the floor.

As the excited buzzing of voices died away, the little Queen announced, "I shall make one more try to find Toto with the Magic Picture, but first I want to see just how far the picture will go. Maybe it is getting weak and he could be out of range. Just a little bit further, this time. Let us see the Scarecrow."

And there he was, Dorothy's first companion in her adventures in Oz, strolling across the lawn in front of his unique mansion. It was shaped and colored like an immense ear of corn! Behind it could be seen row upon row of living corn, growing, and beyond that oats, both to provide bran to stuff his head and straw to stuff his body. From his undistinguished position on a beanpole in a Munchkin field, he had come to be one of the brightest personalities in Oz, living in this magnificent multistoried home.

As they watched, he stepped out into the road in front of his home and headed west. "I'll bet he's headed for the Tin Woodman's," said Dorothy, and the others agreed.

# Toto and the Cats of Oz

Satisfied that it was working this far, Ozma asked to see several more locations, each one further away, until finally she had seen quite clearly all the way across the Nonestic Ocean.

Nodding her head slowly, the young Queen said, "Everything else is working fine, so now we shall try for Toto once more."

Speaking to the Picture again, she said, "Let me see Toto," but as before, only zigzag lines and flashing lights met the gaze of the assembled group.

Shaking her head, the puzzled Queen said, "I don't know what we are going to do about that picture, but at least we can bring Toto back from wherever he is with the Magic Belt," and she walked over to a spot before the west wall of the room. There she muttered a brief magic phrase and a drawer popped out of the wall. From it she removed an enormous jewel-studded belt which she quickly fastened around her waist. A hush fell upon all who were there as, in clear words, she spoke: "Bring Toto to me."

# Chapter 4

# The Failure of Magic

 s the seconds ticked by, everyone waited hopefully. Nothing happened. Ozma repeated, "Bring Toto to me." Again, nothing. After a third attempt and a longer wait, Ozma finally said, "I guess the Magic Belt is not going to work either. I do not really know what to do next."

"Couldn't you send someone to wherever Toto is?" asked Betsy Bobbin.

"I could try, but the way things have been working, that might just cause us to lose someone else".

These alarming words returned silence to the room until the Wizard spoke up with an almost cheerful voice, saying, "No need to lose hope. My workshop is full of appliances. One of them will certainly lead us straight to Toto."

Just then the door opened and in came a man in the white outfit of a cook. With a simple bow, he said, "Your Highness, dinner will soon be ready. Should I prepare for all of you to eat together in the Dining Room?"

"You guessed quite right, Baluol," Ozma replied. "Thank you for asking. We really need to eat together today. Make things ready and we will all be down in just a few minutes."

As the head chef of the Palace left, the Wizard said, "In the meantime, I'll take the Shaggy Man along to help me, and we will soon have this whole thing settled."

"All right," answered the Queen. "That sounds like a good idea. While you two are at work, the rest of us will go down to start on dinner." Then she added with an optimism she did not feel, "When you bring back Toto we will turn it into a big party."

While the Wizard and the Shaggy Man went to the Wizard's workshop, the rest—men, women, children and animals—all trooped down to the dining hall. Usually the gatherings in this great hall were occasions of gaiety, but this time there was little laughter and the voices were subdued. What conversation there was concerned Toto and the mysterious failure of Ozma's magic. Some were even pessimistic as to whether the Wizard could be any more successful than Ozma's magic had been.

When, at last, he came through the door, Tik-Tok was the first to see him. The metallic man started to announce the Wizard's entrance, but before he could finish his sentence, all was hubbub. With much clatter, everyone dropped silver and food back upon his plate and rushed to hear what the Wizard and the Shaggy Man had found.

At first there was a babble of voices, but as the Wizard began to speak all fell silent.

"I'm sorry, but I had no luck. Nothing in my workshop would give me the slightest clue about what became of

# The Failure of Magic

Toto. I just cannot understand it."

"Maybe Oz is getting like America—no magic any more," declared the Wooden Sawhorse.

"Oh, now," answered Uncle Henry, "you know better than that. It was easier than pullin' a bucket o' air out o' the well for us to see all kinds o' things in the Magic Picture."

"It showed us an-y-thing we asked for ex-cept To-to," added Tik-Tok.

"Yes, and it was the same in the Wizard's lab," said the Shaggy Man. "Whatever we tried worked perfectly as long as we did not try to find Toto. Most of our magic works just fine."

"That's right." The little Queen spoke up for the first time. "The magic of our land will never just fade away. No, our problem is something else. I've been thinking. Somehow Toto has been made invulnerable to magic. The only way we're going to find him is to go out on foot and look with our eyes."

Immediately every voice there cried out, practically in chorus, "Let me go. Let me go."

Ozma's serious face broke momentarily into a laugh as she answered, "Not all of us can go. Some must stay here and some must go in search parties. I will go to confer with Glinda, and while I am away, the Wizard will be in charge here in the Emerald City. Those of you who stay here are to obey him as you would me, and when necessary, help him with decisions, just as though it were me."

With a little bow of his head, the Wizard accepted

the responsibility.

Then Ozma began the job of deciding who should go where. Her plan was a good one. The whole of the Land of Oz would be covered by search parties. The central part, spreading around the Emerald City, was easy enough to account for. Mostly it was rolling hills and grassy meadows. Parts of this were just open country that belonged to everyone in the Land of Oz – parks and such, some well kept, others preserved in a wild state. But much of it was beautiful and well-tended farmlands with their pastures, cultivated lands and wood lots that are so typical of all the more civilized areas of the five countries of Oz.

There was nothing very complicated in this great, green central area, and there the search would go quite easily. However, the other four countries were much larger and presented all kinds of unexpected surprises. Great, unexplored forests and wastelands were found in each of them. Off the main roads, one would often come upon strange people, unacquainted with the rules of ordinary folk in Oz and who may not even know that Ozma was the Ruler of Oz. No telling what might be found in these out of the way places. However, in each country, the main population was made up of such people as farmers and tradesmen scattered across the land. At least, among them the search for Toto should go fairly smoothly.

Besides the Emerald City, there were the Winkies to the west; on the south, the Quadlings; to the east, the Munchkins; and in the north, the Gillikins. All five

# The Failure of Magic

countries, together, were enclosed by the impassable barrier of the yellow sands of the Deadly Desert. The touch of these sands would bring death to any unwary person who should chance to walk upon them. It is the combination of this desert and a spell of invisibility which has kept most outsiders from finding Oz.

Those who do reach it find that each country in this great fairyland is easily recognized by its own predominant color group. In the Emerald City, the favorite color for buildings, clothing and nearly everything else is green. In the Munchkin Country they prefer blue; among the Quadlings, red; the Winkies, yellow; and the Gillikins choice is purple.

Of course, even with one color predominating in each country, the gay and colorful Land of Oz could not possibly be content with the monotony of a single range of color. Not only is there a variety of shades, tones and hues everywhere, but also part of every landscape contains a scattering of other colors.

Children in the Munchkin Country, like all the children of Oz, enjoy all the various flavors of Oz Cream, but their most special treat is blueberry Oz Cream. And, whenever carnivals and circuses visit the Munchkins, they are always prepared to sell extra large quantities of blue cotton candy.

Among the Quadling children, watermelons and strawberry shortcake are their favorites. Most surprising of all is the fact that in the Emerald City the children prefer eating green beans and peas and spinach, although they also like a good green apple pie. Their mothers, however, like all good mothers everywhere, caution their children about eating green apples from the trees.

To the west, in Winkie Land, butterscotch pudding and lemonade can be counted on in every home, and up among the Gillikins, grape soda and plum pie are always favored.

From such delicious thoughts, we must return to Ozma's organizing of search parties. She had decided that she would take Scraps with her to the south, riding in the Red Wagon behind the speedy Sawhorse. Surely, Glinda's Magic Record Book could tell them something of what had happened to Toto. In any case, she felt certain that the great Sorceress would be able to provide valuable assistance.

The matter seemed settled until Uncle Henry spoke up: "Now, ya know, I think I just oughta take that trip down to Glinda's too, don't you?" He was speaking slowly, in the way he did when he intended to have his way. "Sure an' there's room for me in that there wagon."

"Of course," laughed Ozma, and with more of humor than of certainty, she added, "I'm sure we would be safe enough, but you can come along just for the joy of the outing." And she laughed again.

Before long, all the search parties were assigned, so everyone went off to his or her own apartment to prepare for the morrow. Dorothy would have liked for her group to start its search for Toto immediately, but, much as it irked her, she knew that there were still many decisions to be made and necessary supplies to organize. Still, when morning came, she chaffed at all the time the

# The Failure of Magic

preparations were taking.

Finally, just a little past noon, amidst the crowds who had come to cheer them on, the search parties began to gather. Dorothy felt as if she had been on the steps for hours. Her own party, consisting of herself, the Cowardly Lion, Button-Bright, Sir Hokus of Pokes and the Hungry Tiger, was already mounted, when the clatter of the Sawhorse's hoofs rang out on the green pavement. Then he came around the corner pulling his Red Carriage with Uncle Henry in it, and just as the two of them came into sight, Ozma and Scraps came out of the great front doors of the palace. The Patchwork Girl stood on tiptoe and called out:

"Here we are, all ready to ride;
Mounted and stirruped, dressed and tied.
Some have come and are just sitting,
Others, here, are still arriving.
All have questions they are asking.
Where is Toto? No one knows.

We have looked both high and low.
Where did our companion go?
Somewhere in this world he's hidden
By some evil quite unbidden.
Fear we must not, for we'll find him.
Come my friends. Away we go!"

With that she somersaulted down the stairs, landing with a plop behind Uncle Henry. Ozma came, not only

# Toto and the Cats of Oz

more slowly, but also more gracefully. When she reached the carriage, she mounted its steps, then standing in the back of it, she addressed the gathered crowd. Speaking quickly and quietly, she told of the purpose of the journeys about to be undertaken and reminded all of them that the Wizard would be in charge until her return. Then, with a word to their steeds, all were off.

The speed of the Sawhorse enabled Ozma's party to complete its journey in only a little over an hour. Clattering up to the gates of Glinda's red palace, the four were astonished to see the front doors open and Glinda, herself, running out to meet them. Her usual quiet way was gone as she cried out:

"Oh, thank goodness! Ozma! I wasn't sure what might be happening. Hurry! Come. See what the Great Book of Records just wrote!"

# Chapter 5

# Toto

ith such unusual happenings in the Emerald City, it would be easy to overlook one horse-drawn wagon on a Munchkin back road. But, if there were no other reason to notice it, our interest would, no doubt, be aroused by the wild speed with which it moved.

It was an old buckboard driven by a large, rough-looking man who guided his horses with the skill and the tender hands of long experience. The six horses were all of the very best quality, but the buckboard was just the opposite. No one could tell how it might originally have been made, but now it was jury-rigged of spare pieces of lumber, mismatched and unpainted or faded. It was packed full of various boxes, packages, bags and one cage, tightly wedged in. For the added security of the contents, ropes crisscrossed the whole thing.

The driver sat jauntily upon the seat clothed in various clashing articles of clothing, singing:

"Ho! The Holder am I,
And I hold what I hold,

# Toto and the Cats of Oz

For any who want something held.

To my caves you may come,
Or to you I will drive.
Whichever, still safe it will be.

On each cave are two doors,
On each door are three locks,
The better to hold it secure!

Here six Kalidahs brave
That stay in my cave
Will hold what you have from all harm.

Ho! The Holder of Oz, I am, that I am!"

Considering that it was a back road and seldom used this old road was really in quite good condition. But, the wagon carried four passengers, quite unknown to the Holder. Four mice, quite unbidden by him, had hopped into the wagon while he was busy with the horses. Then from that time to this, they had been busily chewing at the stout ropes holding that cage in place. The Holder, however, was so occupied with his driving and rollicking singing that he was quite unaware of their mission to thwart his purposes.

At last, the ropes were loose, just as a sharp double curve appeared in the road. Although the driver maneuvered through it with great skill, the changing pressures in the bed of the buckboard caused the cage to squirt up between the boxes. It teetered on top for a while, and then rolled out upon the road. At the same time, the four mice hopped out and ran back to the weeds where the cage had fallen. Although tightly padlocked, the impact as it landed was so violent that the bars were sprung and a bedraggled little black dog squeezed out between them.

"Hey, what's going on here?" he cried in a startled voice. "Where am I anyway?" Then with his eyes opening ever wider in a startled expression, he said slowly, almost gasping, "Who am I? How did I get here? I don't remember anything!"

"Well, obviously, you have fallen out of a wagon."

"You are on a road in the Country of the Munchkins in the Land of Oz."

"Your name is Toto."

"We've been helping you."

The four shrill little voices, each answering one of his questions, came almost simultaneously from the bushes by the side of the road.

"Wait now," responded the dog, "You're only confusing me all the more. None of this makes any sense. If I'm Toto, how come you know it and I don't? And who are you, and where are you?"

Again, the four voices, and again, one after the other:

"We are mice, subjects of Her Royal Highness, Ramina, Queen of the Field Mice."

"She sent us along to release you from your captivity."

"Magic keeps you from knowing your own name."

"And we are right here." The last words were

pronounced as four pert little gray mice stepped out of the bushes.

"You will have to forgive me, but I still don't know what's going on." And with those words, the little black dog sat down and scratched behind his left ear. "You know me, and apparently I should know you, but right now I don't seem to, so why not introduce yourselves?"

"I'm Tish, and these are my sisters and brother."

"I'm Trish."

"I'm Tash."

"And I'm Tank. I'm the biggest."

And now that he really looked closer, the dog could see that the last one was somewhat bigger than the other three and that his voice was deeper, or at least it was not

*. . . four pert little gray mice stepped out of the bushes.*

quite so shrill as the others.

The conversation continued as it started. It seemed that if anything was to be said, all four mice had to have a part in saying it. Thus, speaking in sequence, they explained to Toto how, although he was now a permanent resident of the Emerald City in Oz, he had originally come from America with a little girl named Dorothy. When they first arrived, they had many adventures with three new friends, the Scarecrow, the Tin Woodman and the Cowardly Lion. During one of these adventures, the three members of the traveling group who were flesh and blood had been overcome by the fragrance of the Deadly Poppy Field, and the mice had helped save them.

"That's when we first saw you."

"We were four out of thousands that pulled the Cowardly Lion out."

"And we have seen you from time to time since then."

"But you don't seem to remember any of that, do you?"

"No," replied the dog, Toto, "it's all a blank to me, but I suppose I should go back to this Emerald City you mention and see if the friends you tell me of can set me straight."

"We would go with you."

"But, having saved you, we have another duty to perform for our Queen."

"We have a message for Boq, the Munchkin farmer."

"The Emerald City is easy to find though."

"Just follow this road."

"Back down the mountain and along the river."

# Toto and the Cats of Oz

"Until you come to a Yellow Brick Road."

"Then turn left, and follow the Yellow Brick Road to the Emerald City."

After expressing his gratitude for their help, Toto bade the four mice good-bye and started down the road that Trish had pointed out. Soon the predominant blues had turned to red, and in another hour, they had given way to shades of green. Toto wondered about this change in color, but within him, it just seemed right. If his memory had been working, it would have told him that the colors showed when he left the Munchkin Country, passed through a small corner of the Quadling Country, and then entered the large area surrounding the Emerald City.

As dusk was approaching, he decided to lie down to sleep under a small bush a short distance from the road, thinking as he did, *It must have been a hard day. I don't remember anything before I met the mice, but something surely made me tired.*

He slept until the sun was well up the next morning. Then off he went, on toward the Yellow Brick Road and the Emerald City. Soon after reaching that road and turning west upon it, he saw another animal coming down the road toward him from the direction of the city. It was the biggest cat he had ever seen, but then he was not certain he had ever seen a cat before. Something inside him just said, "Cat." And that same thing said, "Chase it." But from the size of it, he was not sure that would be a good idea. If Toto could have remembered more of his past, he would have realized that this truly

# Toto

was a giant of a cat – half alley cat and half wildcat, and bigger and tougher than either.

While he stood there, uncertain about his next move, the cat came within hailing distance and called out, "Hi. 'S that you, Toto?" And still closer, though practically running now, he added, "It's OK. We're on the same side now."

Somewhat reassured, Toto answered, "I guess it's all right. I don't really know. I cannot seem to remember anything before yesterday afternoon."

"Ya don't 'member 'bout all the cats then?"

"No-o-o," Toto said slowly, "I am not even sure what a cat is, but I think that is what you are, isn't it?"

At that the big cat started laughing. He laughed and laughed. Then practically choking, he said, "Yeah. I'm a cat. Let me introduce myself. I'm Alexander. And yesterday I, uh, yesterday was the first time I'd ever seen the Emerald City."

"And I guess," said Toto, "that until yesterday, I had lived in the Emerald City."

"Well, I've a lot t' tell ya 'bout that, but c'mon kid, let's get goin'. Best we get away from the main roads." And off he went toward the south.

"Wait a minute," said Toto. "The mice told me I should go to the Emerald City where my friends are, and they would help me in every way."

"That was OK yesterday, but today your friends've all left the City."

"What do you mean? Where did they go?"

"Well, some went south an' some went west an' some

went north an' some went east. But believe me, there's trouble between here an' there. An' I understand there's a good witch in the south that can help us."

"Yes," responded Toto, "She is, ah-h. Hmm, G-, G-. Hunh. It's right there someplace, but I can't really remember. I guess maybe you're right. We'll go south."

Not far ahead of them was a forest covering the foothills as well as the slopes of the more distant mountains. As they traveled together, Toto began getting better acquainted with Alexander. The cat, it developed, was also from America. He had only been in Oz for ten days, but he thought it the most wonderful place in the world.

"Wow! Everything's so different! There's magic aroun' every corner and here I even talk with people ... an', an' with you. Why back in America we would'a been deadly enemies!"

"Is that so? Well then, why should I believe that we are friends now?"

Towering above Toto and smiling down upon him the big cat laughed, "It kind'a looks t' me like ya'd better."

Catching the humor of Alexander, and knowing he would be completely outclassed in any fight with that cat, Toto responded, "I see what you mean, but what about people? You and the mice have both mentioned them. I seem to remember ... we'd play and talk ... I think ...."

"That's right. Y're with 'em all 'a time."

"H-m, I can almost .... That's strange! You know, I haven't seen any since I fell out of that wagon, but I seem to know what you mean—tall, two-legged, hardly any fur, cover themselves with cloth instead. Is that right?"

"Sure. Ya got the idea OK."

"Good. Some things seem to be coming back … a little anyway. I guess that Dorothy, Ozma, the Tin Woodman, the Scarecrow and the Wizard that the mice told me about are people, right?"

"Right … more or less."

"Good," said Toto. "I have that much clear, but what about you? The mice explained about magic, and according to them, that's what it took for me to get from America to Oz, but since magic is new to you, how did you make the trip?"

At that Alexander stammered a little nervously. "Well, ah-h, yeah. That's the point. It is new t' me. One minute I was sittin' quietly on a pier in Seattle, the next, I was in blue grass in the Land of Oz. Some magical cat here in Oz had brought me over … I don't know how."

"Hm-m, a magical cat? What was his name?"

Still a bit unnerved, Alexander muttered, "Um-m, ah-h, Joom."

"Joom," Toto mouthed the word carefully. "It seems to me that his name means something to me."

Hurriedly, the cat said, "Yup, I'm sure it does, but we c'n talk about that later. Right now we gotta find a path."

They had come to the forest, and he was right. They could easily get lost if they were not following a regular trail, but at this time what was most important to Alexander was to get off the subject of the other cat—Joom.

# Chapter 6

# The Pumpkin House

n the previous day, long before Toto was saying "Good-bye" to the mice, the various search parties had been saying, "Good-bye," to their friends in the Emerald City. The group made up of Dorothy, Button-Bright, the Cowardly Lion, the Hungry Tiger and Sir Hokus had headed west toward Jack Pumpkinhead's. It was evening by the time they reached his quaint home.

Despite the hours that had passed since they had seen him in the Magic Picture, Jack was still standing in his empty pumpkin patch—acres and acres of pumpkin vines, but no pumpkins. Seeing his friends approaching, he wailed, "My pumpkins, my pumpkins! The cats have taken them all. Oh, my pumpkins!"

"Yes, we saw," said Dorothy.

"We were watching in the Magic Picture," put in Button-Bright.

"And why thinkest thou it was cats?" asked Sir Hokus.

"Yes," continued the Cowardly Lion. "One moment your field was full of pumpkins and the next, they were gone with no sign of who did it."

# The Pumpkin House

"What do you mean? No sign! Indeed! There were cats all over the place — black ones, gray ones, white ones, yellow ones, big ones, little ones — all kinds. And each of them took one of my pumpkins after quickly hollowing it out."

"That's right!" exclaimed Button-Bright. "I 'member seein' little piles of seeds an' stuff stacking up next to each pun'kin, just like when Jack makes them into pies. Then, after all the seeds were out, then the pun'kins disappeared."

"You mean it was like Jack said?" asked Dorothy.

"Well, I didn't see any cats, but someone was tossin' the insides out just before the pun'kins disappeared,' said Button-Bright.

"There. You said it again," wailed Jack. "They didn't just disappear. The cats took them and ran away with them!"

"Goodness," declared Dorothy, "we saw no cats in the Magic Picture. It must have gone haywire."

"Methinks that would'st not be hard to believe after the other skullduggery it has fooled us with, M'lass!" exclaimed Sir Hokus.

"Skullduggery? What's happened?" Jack asked anxiously.

And so, explanations were shared. First, Dorothy and her traveling companions told about Toto's disappearance. Then, when Jack said he'd seen nothing of Toto, they went on to tell about the failure of the Magic Picture, the Magic Belt and the Wizard's magic.

Once their tale was told, Jack shook his head. "I've

never heard of such a thing. And now these cats running off with my pumpkins! What do you make of it?"

"Demons! That's what 'tis," answered the knight. "There are demons and hobgoblins out to do us in. Yea verily, this quest becomes darker by the nonce."

"The day darkens as well," said the Cowardly Lion, "and if there are demons and hobgoblins out to get us, I think we'd better go inside."

"Oh, you are right. Forgive me," apologized the Pumpkinhead. "Won't you all come in and stay the night with me?"

"Thought you'd never ask," laughed Dorothy.

"When it gets dark, I get hungry," added the Tiger.

"Aw, you're always hungry," Button-Bright responded. "'Sides, you have plenty of food in your saddlebags."

As they all moved toward Jack's house, Dorothy explained to their host that they would have to leave early in the morning to continue looking for Toto. Although Jack, being made of wood, never ate nor slept, he was accustomed to having those who did as visitors, so he was well prepared. There never was anything fancy about eating at his place, but there always was plenty to eat, and this night it was just the right kinds of food for boys and girls, and questing knights, and lions and tigers. After dinner, Jack showed them to their rooms. He had even prepared one large room with a pile of straw for the comfort of the two cats.

Now, Jack's home was equipped like any other Winkie home. Its color was even like that found in some of them—orange. But it certainly did not look like

# The Pumpkin House

any other Winkie house, for it was made of something different. It was made entirely of pumpkins. At the center was one of the most immense pumpkins ever grown, and connected to it were other extremely large ones serving as bedrooms, store rooms and the like.

Although Jack grew all kinds of pumpkins in various shades, shapes and sizes, there was no way he, himself, could grow one even as large as the smallest of these side rooms. No, that required the help of an old friend, Dr. Pipt, whose Powder of Life had brought Scraps and Bungle to life. He had gotten the formula for it from another magician, Dr. Nikidik whose original batch had brought Jack and the Wooden Sawhorse to life.

The practice of magic was forbidden in the Land of Oz except for a few trusted friends Ozma could count on to use their power for good. Dr. Pipt, who was also known as the Crooked Magician, was one of these. His nickname did not mean he was dishonest, but it was because his long hours of stirring pots had so badly bent his body out of its normal shape.

It is true that at one time Ozma had barred him from practicing magic and the Wizard had straightened out his crooked joints. However, they soon found that he knew so much about magical formulas and the mixing of miraculous brews that he could be of more help to them practicing magic than refraining from it. He really loved his work and would sometimes spend weeks bending over deep kettles, stirring and mixing and mumbling to himself. It was not unusual to find him using both hands and both feet for stirring, and even, on occasion, he would hold a fifth one in his mouth. Of course this last spoon could not last for very long. Sooner or later, his wife, Margolotte, would interrupt him, insisting that he eat something other than the handle of a spoon. Such long hours of stirring had their effect on the old magician and now he was as bent and misshapen as ever he had been before Ozma and the Wizard had first straightened him out.

Every few years, Jack found it necessary to call on the good Dr. Pipt to place some of his Peerless Expansion Enhancing Compound in a few of the pumpkins. This was the cause of their unbelievable size. Then, when they were ready, Jack would carefully hollow them out. With equal care, he would cut doors and windows where he wanted them. Finally, he would season them and dry them so that they would last as long as possible. Thus, after several months, he would have a new pumpkin ready to replace the old one that was weakening with age. This process always did something special to the fragrance of Jack's home. Upon entering it, one might think that he had walked into grandma's while she was baking pumpkin pie.

As you might expect, with such delicious aromas all about, Button-Bright was up early and hungry. He stretched a few moments, and then, dressing in haste, hurried out to the kitchen. Jack was already there, and knowing the effect upon little boys and girls of a night's sleep in his house, he already had some good hot pumpkin pies coming out of the oven.

"Now, none of this until you have had your oatmeal

and milk," he warned Button-Bright.

"Aw shucks," responded the boy, stopping right beside them.

"Don't worry," continued Jack. "These pies are too hot to eat right now anyway. OK?"

"OK. But let me help," offered Button-Bright.

"Good. You can set out the plates and silverware for the three of you while I get some meat out of the freezer for the Hungry Tiger and the Cowardly Lion."

"When're they all getting up?" the boy asked, looking anxiously toward those tantalizing pumpkin pies.

"If they're not up by the time I bring in the animal's food, you may go get them."

"Hurray! Let's hurry!" cried Button-Bright enthusiastically.

"You will have to hurry pretty fast," growled a voice behind him. Startled, the youngster turned quickly and was almost enveloped in a large, wide open mouth full of big, sharp teeth. "I'm hungry!" the voice growled as its teeth snapped shut inches from Button-Bright's nose.

"Oh, you don't scare me, you silly old Tiger," and Button-Bright swung himself smoothly up onto the great beast's back.

"Why not?"

"I don't know," was the only answer as the child proceeded to scratch behind the ears of the Hungry Tiger and bury his head in its fur.

Immediately the Hungry Tiger began purring — a sound you or I might easily have mistaken for a growl, but Button-Bright knew what it was.

51

# Toto and the Cats of Oz

*"I'm hungry!" the voice growled . . .*

By this time the others were gathering, and as
Dorothy began to set the table, her young friend jumped
off the Tiger's back saying, "Hey, wait. That's my job. I'm
helping Jack."

"Where is he?" Dorothy asked.

Licking his chops, the Tiger replied, "He's getting
meat for the Cowardly Lion and me."

"Oof, that is a big job," mused Dorothy. "Maybe I had
better go help him."

"Oh no," came the voice of Sir Hokus as he entered
the room. "Fie upon me if I should'st allow yon tender
maiden to carry such a burden! 'Tis my knightly duty.
Allow me, fair Dorothy."

# The Pumpkin House

"Of course," she replied, "but I'll still come along, just for the fun of it."

When they returned, breakfast was ready and all six sat down around the table. Jack, of course, was not eating, but he took his part in the lively conversation as decisions were made about the day's activities.

All but the Pumpkinhead and Button-Bright were to leave right after breakfast, heading for the Tin Woodman's. Jack would stay behind to clean up his pumpkin field, and Button-Bright would stay to help — or maybe just to enjoy the antics of his old friend. If they found Toto, the search party would come by Jack's house on their way back to the Emerald City. If they should not show up within the few days it would take Jack to get his new pumpkins planted, he and Button-Bright would go to the Emerald City to find out what was happening.

Now breakfast was over and everybody was ready to go. "Good-byes" were said all around and the four were soon off on their journey with fresh supplies in their dinner pails.

# Chapter 7

# The Tin Castle

oming over a slight rise in the prairie through which they had been traveling, the two great beasts stopped, awestruck. Normally, the trip from Jack's to the Tin Woodman's would have been only a matter of a long morning's ride, but this time they had wandered between the highway and the Winkie River, checking to see if they could find any sign of Toto. Their search had been fruitless and had also delayed them until now it was well into the night. Not far before them, appeared the great Tin Palace of Nick Chopper, Emperor of all the Winkies.

Originally a man of flesh like everyone else, Nick Chopper had been a simple wood-cutter in one of the great blue forests of the Munchkin Country. He had fallen in love with a beautiful girl who was the slave of the Wicked Witch of the East. When the evil old crone found out about their love, she enchanted the Woodman's ax so that it would slip and cut him. Every time he lost a limb in this way, he would go to his friend, the tinsmith, and have a replacement made of tin. Since no one in Oz can die, this went on until all his parts had been

# The Tin Castle

replaced, and the flesh and blood woodman had become one completely made of tin.

Although tin does not rust, the screws holding his joints together were made of iron, and once, when he was caught in the rain, they rusted, holding him in a rigid stance for about a year. Finally, when Dorothy was on her first trip to Oz, she found him, quite unexpectedly, and rescued him. Together with the Cowardly Lion, the Scarecrow and Toto they went through many adventures, including destroying the Wicked Witch of the West. The Winkies were so grateful for this and so fond of the shiny Tin Woodman that they made him their Emperor, and he has ruled them well and wisely ever since.

In honor of their beloved ruler, the Winkies had long ago built him a new castle of tin to replace the old and dangerously damp one of stone in which the old witch had lived.

Even from a distance the bright lights shining upon the polished tin walls made them gleam with great beauty. As a matter of fact, seeing them from a mile or so added to the fairy-like silvery scene. In all the darkness of the night, here glowed a light to rival that of the moon. The varying angles of the faces of the towers and battlements each reflected a slightly different intensity of light. Each spire and dome seemed almost to have a life of its own.

"It never ceases to thrill me when I come to my old friend's palace after dark," commented the Cowardly Lion. "It's beautiful, shining so in the night."

"Yes, I suppose it is," sighed the Hungry Tiger, "but how can you think of beauty at a time like this when my

55

backbone almost touches the ground from hunger?"

"Oh, it hasn't been so long since we ate."

"Yes it has," the Tiger replied, growling rather loudly. "It has been at least two hours since we had dinner."

"Hush, you will wake the people," objected the Lion.

"Ho now, let there be no disputing among friends," called out Sir Hokus. "M'lady, Dorothy, and I are already awake."

"And enjoying the view," added the young girl. "But we must hurry on. I'm sure it is getting to be quite late."

"I'm afraid you're right," replied the Cowardly Lion as he started trotting toward the castle, "but at least all those lights shining so brightly assure us that plenty of people are still up and around."

"Yes," said Dorothy thoughtfully, "but why would so many lights be burning so late?"

"They must be having some big celebration," said the Hungry Tiger.

"Yea, verily," joined in the knight.

"So there should be food," continued the Hungry Tiger.

By now they were nearing the gates and could hear considerable hubbub from inside. However, it did not seem exactly like the noise of a celebration. As they came nearer, the gates opened for them and they could see a large crowd of Winkies filling the vestibule. It was clear, now, that they were not celebrating. They were disturbed about something. There were far more of them than would usually be found around the castle. Seeing the travelers, the crowds moved toward them.

# The Tin Castle

Their attitude seemed rather ominous to the Cowardly Lion who whispered, "I-I'm s-scared."

"N'er a hair of Princess Dorothy's head shall be harmed as long as I stand," cried Sir Hokus as he jumped off the Tiger's back. Unfortunately, his eagerness and the weight of his own armor were too great for him and sent him sprawling upon the ground.

As she tried to help him up, Dorothy cautioned, "Wait now. Can't you hear what they're saying?"

By this time, both of the animals were crouched and ready to spring, but they paused to listen, and now they, too, could hear certain voices rising above the uproar.

"Our cats! They have all disappeared!"

"No one has seen a cat anyplace in the country of the Winkies for the past two days."

"A delegation is in discussing it with the Emperor right now."

"It is not right. It just is not right. Something is quite wrong."

"The Scarecrow is there too."

"Surely you bring us help from the Emerald City."

Voice piled upon voice until Dorothy raised her hand to silence the bedlam. "We know little more than you do except that yesterday morning Jack Pumpkinhead's fields were full of cats."

"But we do not know where they went from there," added the Cowardly Lion, "and when we were watching the pumpkin fields in the Magic Picture, the cats did not show up on it at all."

Frantically, a voice from the crowd of Winkies cried

# Toto and the Cats of Oz

out, "I told you it was not right."

"Forsooth, it is even worse," declared the knight, "for the dog, Toto, has disappeared too, and naught could be done, even by the magic of Ozma or the Tin Wizard, to locate him!"

At that announcement, many surprised exclamations and a babble of questions came from the crowd. Soon however, the travelers from the Emerald City could see that no one knew any more about these mysterious happenings than did they themselves.

Word of their arrival went ahead of them, and even as they were moving toward the center of the palace, they could hear a clatter coming toward them. Around the corner, came the Tin Woodman, the Tin Soldier and the Scarecrow, hurrying to greet their old friends and to share with them this latest mystery of the disappearance of the cats. Before they could speak, Dorothy was rushing toward them, sobbing.

"Oh Nick, Scarecrow, it's so good to see you again, and you too, Captain Fyter!" Then, throwing her arms around the Tin Woodman, she continued sobbing out her story. "It's so terrible. Even Ozma's and the Wizard's magic can't find Toto! And he's been with me so long, and I don't know what I'll do, and …. What will he do without me?"

"That's OK, Dorothy dear. We'll help you find him," comforted the Scarecrow.

"But please, be careful," Captain Fyter broke in, "your tears will rust the Emperor's neck."

"Now that's all right," comforted the Tin Woodman.

# The Tin Castle

*"Oh Nick, Scarecrow, it's so good to see you again . . ."*

"My oil can is handy and you need those tears right now, but tell us what's happened."

Between the Lion, the Tiger, the Princess and the Knight, the story of the failure of magic was soon told. When they had finished, the Scarecrow, with deliberate thoughtfulness, began talking: "The cats do not show up in the Magic Picture. Toto does not show up. But everything else does. Ozma's Picture has never failed like this before. All the cats have left! And why? To hollow out pumpkins and disappear!"

"Jack could see them, but we could not," said Dorothy.

"Yea verily!" exclaimed Sir Hokus. "But what is to be done?"

# Toto and the Cats of Oz

"Let me think," replied the Scarecrow as they entered the Throne Room where he draped himself over a chair. One could not fairly say he sat upon it, for his posture would have looked most awkward to you and me. But, for a man made only of old clothes stuffed with straw, it was quite natural. One of his legs wound around a leg of the chair with his body twisted and leaning quite precariously over the chair back, while one hand reached through the slats and round behind the chair to scratch his head. A comical sight indeed, but in this serious moment all remained silent while the Scarecrow thought.

Finally he spoke up again: "You said you were to report back to the Emerald City when you had found everything you possibly could. Well, I think you have found all that you can for now, so let us head back."

"But there is so much of the Winkie Country we have not yet searched," objected Dorothy.

"Ah yes," rejoined the stuffed man. "However, right here are Winkies from all over this country who know it well and can search it much more quickly and thoroughly than we few can."

"What is more," broke in the Emperor, "they are already so upset about their missing cats that they will gladly scour every corner. With as many as we have here, I am certain they can cover all of Winkieland for us within a couple days."

"Oh, that's just wonderful!" exclaimed Dorothy. "If all the other search parties Ozma has sent out can be this fortunate, I am sure we can find Toto and the cats too."

"Forsooth," spoke up the knight. "'Tis right. E'en so, another band did the good Queen Ozma send into this Winkie Country's southern part. They may already have some good tidings."

"Could you show us where to find them?" asked the Tin Woodman.

"Within certain bounds, I vow."

"Then Captain Fyter will take you to find maps and you can, no doubt, locate their routes."

With that, the two men clanked off—one encased in metal and the other made of metal. It is strange to say, but the history of Captain Fyter had been much the same as that of Nick Chopper. Soon after the disappearance and rusting of the Tin Woodman, one of the flesh and blood soldiers in the Wicked Witch's guard had fallen in love with the same girl, Nimmie Amee. This was Captain Fyter, and when the witch found out that now she was in love with this soldier, she bewitched his sword, just as she had Nick Chopper's ax—and with quite the same results. Only this time, it was not Dorothy who came along, but the Tin Woodman who rescued the Tin Soldier from an eternity of rust. Having so much in common, the two had become close friends.

While the Tin Soldier and Sir Hokus went to look for maps, the others continued making their plans. Winkies would be dispatched in the morning to intercept the other search party and to cover every remaining corner of the country within the next two days. At the same time Dorothy, Sir Hokus, the Cowardly Lion, the

Hungry Tiger, the Tin Woodman, the Tin Soldier and the Scarecrow would return to Jack Pumpkinhead's on the way to the Emerald City.

Men of tin and straw do not sleep, but the others, who had become very tired with all this late night activity, were ushered to special quarters where they could sleep until morning, never dreaming of the strange adventure that awaited them the next day.

# Chapter 8

# An Amazing Bee

reak of dawn the next day found the Tin Woodman, the Tin Soldier and the Scarecrow busily making preparations in the kitchen. Although they, themselves, would require no food, they knew that the people and animals would. However, they had only made a good start at putting the lunches together when Dorothy and Sir Hokus fairly flew into the kitchen.

"He couldn't sleep any longer and neither could I," Dorothy called out as she came through the doorway. "Come on let's be on our way."

"But we hardly have any food ready for you yet," said the Tin Woodman.

"That's all right. You can get enough packed for us while we eat breakfast. I'll go get the Lion and the Tiger now."

"And 'twill be my joyful duty," proudly spoke he who was once of Pokes, "thy breakfast to prepare whilst thou art gone."

It did not take long to gather, eat, pack and put the seven of them on their way. Because of the early breakfast,

# Toto and the Cats of Oz

lunch came early too. The others might have waited a while longer, but the Hungry Tiger just could not bear to delay eating any longer. Then again, in mid-afternoon, he insisted on stopping for dinner. As he licked up the last crumbs, he moaned, "Now look at that, we will not have another thing to eat until we reach Jack's. I will never make it."

"I'm sorry about that," replied the Tin Woodman. "We have slowed you down."

"Oh, it's not so bad," mumbled the Tiger. "I would rather have my friends with me and be a bit hungry than to be full and alone."

None the less his complaints were soon renewed and ignored by the others, all quite use to them, until, after what seemed like the hundredth time, the Tin Soldier laughed and said, "Oh stop it. You are making me hungry" — a thing, of course, quite impossible for this man of tin.

"You're always Hungry," added Dorothy to the feline. "That's your first name."

"Well, it may be his first name, but it is not mine," said the Cowardly Lion. "And I am getting hungry myself. I think it's time we started looking. There would probably be something to eat in those woods."

Trotting across a little meadow by the side of the road, the two big cats stopped under the nearest tree to let their riders off. After doing so, they had only taken a couple of steps into the woods when they were pulled up short by a cry from Dorothy: "Ick! I'm sticking to this tree."

# An Amazing Bee

Sure enough. She had leaned against a big old oak, and now, as she pulled away from it, a great mass of honey trailed behind her.

"Thanks. That is good enough for me," said the Lion as he wiped the honey from Dorothy's back with his tongue.

"Me too," and the Tiger pounced up to reach into the cavity from which the honey was dripping. Then for several minutes the great beasts busied themselves, dragging out paws full of honey and purring their contentment.

"Um-muha," and the Lion was about to take one more mouthful when, suddenly, the Tin Woodman came hurtling through the air, calling out, "Stop! Stop! Don't eat him!"

And there, in the mass of honey in his old friend's paws, was the largest bee anyone had ever seen. Despite his size, there was so much honey that he was thoroughly imprisoned, struggling weakly in the sticky mess.

Forgetting the danger to his own tin joints, Nick wiped away as much of the honey as he could without hurting the delicate membranes of the bee's wings. Then, holding him carefully in his arms, he took him to a near-by stream and let the water wash away the last of the sweetly clinging honey.

Looking quite bedraggled, with water dripping from every joint and angle of his great body, the Bee said, "Whew! Thank you, you marvelous tin man. To think, I was almost done for!"

Everyone just stood and looked at this outsize bee for

# Toto and the Cats of Oz

*And there . . . was the largest bee anyone had ever seen.*

awhile. Finally Dorothy, amazed at the sight, said, "Why even in Oz, I never expected to see a bee as large as you!"

"How did you get so big?" asked the Scarecrow.

"Harrumph, I just do not remember. It seems to me that I have always been this big."

"Do you sting?" the Cowardly Lion asked in a quavering voice.

"Oh goodness, no. I am not a stinging bee, I am a Spelling Bee."

"Spelling Bee?" laughed the travelers, and Captain Fyter challenged it to spell kaleidoscope.

"Kaleidoscope, k-a-l-e-i-d-o-s-c-o-p-e, kaleidoscope,"

# An Amazing Bee

recited the Bee, rapidly,."It means 'a complex, colorful shifting pattern, and that's just a beginning. Wait 'til you hear me cast a spell!"

"Thou canst cast spells!" exclaimed Sir Hokus.

"Can you cast a spell to get rid of my hunger?" asked the big Tiger.

"Of course I can," and with mysterious magical gestures of both sets of hands and his antennae, he chanted:

"F-i-l-l-e-d-u-p.
This spell I cast, now let it be,
All hunger gone, zu-del-lif-gup.
The Tiger now is all filled up."

"Oh! You cannot do that," cried Dorothy. "That's magic, and all magic is strictly forbidden unless it is approved by Ozma."

"Harrumph, yes. I keep forgetting. Anyway, it's all right. I never hurt anyone with one of my spells." Then, a bit hesitantly, he added, "I don't think so anyway."

By this time the Hungry Tiger was jumping up and down. "Look at me! I'm not hungry! I just am not even the least bit hungry!"

"Zounds!" exclaimed Sir Hokus. "Dorothy is right. E'en though thy hunger has gone, still, we canst not have people practicing magic all over the place!"

"I'm sorry," said the Bee. "I will try to remember not to cast spells. The only thing is, it all comes to me so naturally, I'm afraid I'll forget to remember."

# Toto and the Cats of Oz

In all this excitement, no one had paid any particular attention to the Tin Woodman, but now the Scarecrow interrupted, "Oh, good grief! Look what has happened to Nick!"

There stood the Emperor of the Winkies, quite motionless, except for his jaws; saying "I am afraid washing the Bee has quite rusted me in place."

"Quick then, the oil can," cried the Tin Soldier with a note of fear in his voice, remembering too clearly his lonely vigil of rust. Already, he had his own can popping away, lubricating all the joints of his friend. As he worked, Dorothy used a cloth to wipe away the sticky honey. Over and over him they went until he was spruced up, shining and moving freely again.

"Thank you once more Dorothy. I have quite lost track of how many times you have brought my limbs back to motion." Then turning to his tin friend, he added, "And thanks too, to you. You are indeed the best of friends."

"And, as you thank them, so I thank you, man of tin," said the great bee. You have most certainly saved me from remaining as immobile as ever you were."

"That's quite all right. What are friends for if not to help one another?" To the bee he said, "No need to call me 'man of tin.' My name is Nick Chopper, although most people call me the Tin Woodman."

"Now, what is your name?" asked Dorothy and the Scarecrow at the same time.

Looking a bit perplexed, their new friend glanced from one to the other and said, "Ah yes, now. That is an odd thing. I never can seem to remember my own name.

# An Amazing Bee

The whole world just calls me 'The Spelling Bee'." At that, everyone laughed.

"I have trouble that way," he continued. "I forget a lot of things, but I never forget a spell. Would you like to see me do one?"

"Ah, ah," warned Dorothy. "No working spells in Oz!"

"Oh yes," he apologized. "I forgot."

"I thought we were in such a hurry!" exclaimed the Hungry Tiger. "No one could spare much time for a stop for my stomach, but now that I'm not so hungry, every one has plenty of time to stand around chitchatting."

"Now, don't be rude to our friend," growled the Cowardly Lion. "We are just getting acquainted. Surely it doesn't hurt you if we take time to rescue a poor bee."

"Argh-h," muttered the Tiger.

Patting the usually Hungry one on the neck, Dorothy said, "You are right, of course. We do have to hurry now." Then, turning to the Bee, she added, "Would you like to travel with us?"

"Well, ah, yes-s," he replied hesitantly, "I think I could do that. I cannot remember anything else I should be doing just now."

"Grant first this boon," requested Sir Hokus, "that first we may fill up on this fine sweet honey."

"Oh, most certainly, most certainly," answered the Bee. "You have saved my life. For such as you, the whole tree can be taken. Help yourselves."

Laughing at the bee's droll expression, Dorothy reached over and dipped her fingers into the sticky mass.

# Toto and the Cats of Oz

During the next few minutes she and the knight and the Lion were busy eating their fill of honey, while the Tiger sat upon his haunches purring, "Look at them eat, and I do not feel the least bit hungry! I am all filled up!"

Finally everyone was ready to be off again. Dorothy clambered to her place upon the Lion's back while the armored knight mounted into his saddle on the back of the Hungry Tiger. Returning to the path, the strange looking procession started toward the Emerald City once more. The giant Bee buzzed along beside his new special friend, the Tin Woodman, talking of this and that. Ahead of them went the Scarecrow and the Tin Soldier. At the back of the column came the two great beasts bearing Dorothy and Sir Hokus. Shoulder to shoulder, their immense bulk took up the entire width of the road.

# Chapter 9

# The Spelling Bee's Story

s the party marched through woods and meadows, they discussed various matters. Although none of the others had ever heard of the Spelling Bee, he knew of the Tin Emperor, the marvelous Scarecrow, the Cowardly Lion and the Hungry Tiger, and had heard that in the Emerald City, Queen Ozma had several friends who came from a strange and distant land, chief among them a little girl named Dorothy.

"I really try to keep pretty much to myself," he said. "You can understand that I would, harrumph, I say I would not really be welcome in an ordinary sized bee-hive. And then again, most people are really quite frightened by my, ah, size. So you see, I lead a rather lonely life."

"What a pity," grieved the Tin Woodman, poking with his oily rag at the sympathetic tears forming in his eyes.

"Now," added Dorothy, "we will be your friends and you don't have to be lonely any more."

"Was it because of being alone so much that some

71

accident overcame you, trapping you in all that honey?" asked the Tin Soldier.

"Mercy no!" replied the Bee. "Oh, it was terrible — my own honey — and there I was, stuck! Oh! Oh! Oh!"

"Yes, but how did it happen?" persisted Captain Fyter.

"It was just yesterday. Ahem. I can tell because it only got dark once. Amazing how much light filters through all that honey. Well, anyway, several days before that, I had made friends with this cat. Oh! That terrible cat!"

"So you have had cat troubles too?" commented the Tin Woodman. "That is what started me out on this trip."

"Oh, have I had cat troubles! You could not guess how much I have had cat troubles," answered the Bee. "This dumb old cat! He did it on purpose!"

"Did what?" rumbled the Tiger.

"Poured all that honey on me."

"How did he do that?" asked Dorothy. "I am getting confused."

"Yea verily," added Sir Hokus. "Surely thy spells woulds't have protected thee."

"Most assuredly," replied the Bee, "if I had only had a chance to use them."

"Start from the beginning again," suggested the Scarecrow.

"All right. Now, let me see. Ah yes, now. How far back should I go? Harrumph, hum. You want to know how that awful cat could pour honey on me with all my magic spells that might have stopped him. Right?"

# The Spelling Bee's Story

"Right," replied the Scarecrow.

"Yes, of course. Well, it all started when this strange cat came to me with the most heart rending story of how a mean old witch was using her magic power to wipe out all the cats in Oz. She was upset over something her own cat had done. So now he feared that his species was doomed to extinction. Heh, extinction! Harrumph, ah, so I asked him why he did not go to Ozma, and he said he would have, but it would take so long and there was no telling how many cats that wicked witch might destroy in the meantime. Humm-humph. Of course I was sympathetic — the poor cats — but when he said that rather than waste time he had come to the 'far famed Spelling Bee' who was so close and so powerful — well, my dears, I am afraid my vanity took over, and I completely overlooked the 'peculiarities' which were soon to occur. 'Powerful,' indeed! More like 'foolish'!"

By this time everyone was thoroughly engrossed in his story and waited patiently while he fluttered around a bit. Then he cleared his throat once more, muttering, "Now where was I? Ah yes. The story of that wicked cat." Then speaking strongly for all to hear once more, he continued, "Of course there was not a word of truth in it, but I did not find that out until later. Oh woe of woes, unfortunately I knew exactly the spell he needed. Oh, if only I had also known what he was up to! But you can understand my desire to help the poor little cats, can't you?"

"We certainly can," responded the Lion and Tiger, with emphasis.

73

# Toto and the Cats of Oz

"It is no more than I would have done," nodded the Tin Woodman as the others added their agreement. Then carefully putting his heavy metal arm around the trembling shoulders of the bee, he continued, "But what could you do?"

"Hah! What could I do? I could do exactly what the cat wanted. Probably no one else in all Oz could have done it. But I could! Oh shame! I never should have done it!"

"Done what?" asked the Scarecrow.

"Oh goodness, goodness, goodness! No, I should say 'Oh, badness, badness, badness!" Look what I have done!" And now the Bee began crying.

The others gathered around as Dorothy took two of the big Bee's hands in her own. After a few minutes his sobs began to subside, and, encouraged by his new friends, he resumed his story. Speaking slowly at first, the more he told of his story, the more animated he became.

"It is really pretty bad. I did not realize what he was up to and I used my Counter-Spell to help him in his evil plans."

"'Counter-Spell?' What's that?" asked the Hungry Tiger.

"Ahem, why yes now. That is a very special spell. It is a spell against spells and all other forms of magic. Um-m-mh, yes. While you are under its influence, no other magic can have any effect upon you whatsoever! I think he must have known all along that I could produce the power of this spell. Hum-nh, yes. Ah, at any rate; pretending that he needed to protect the cats from the

# The Spelling Bee's Story

wickedness of the old witch, the dastardly cat persuaded me to work my Counter-Spell upon them. I followed him into the meadow near where you found me, harrumph, and there I saw the cats. Why, there were more cats and more kinds of cats than I ever imagined existed."

"I know," said the Tine Woodman. "He probably had all the cats from the Winkie Country with him."

"Looking for those cats is part of why we are on this trip," continued Captain Fyter.

"Harrumph. No, I do not think these were the Winkie cats," responded the Spelling Bee. "He brought the cats in three different groups. Yes, I say, in three different groups, each several days apart. Ahem now, there were not many yellow cats until the last. That, oh woe is me, was when I put the spell upon him, too. Yes, indeed, it was after that last group, the Winkie cats, that I discovered I had been tricked into helping a truly dangerous beast."

Warming to his subject and getting more excited, the Bee continued, "When he arrived with that final mob of cats, I was, ahem, yes, I say, I was just about to finish sealing up that whole tree of honey, the one where you found me."

His rapt listeners nodded their understanding and variously said "Yes," "Um-hm," "Quite."

The Bee continued, "I interrupted the sealing job long enough to put the Counter-Spell on those cats. And when I was done with that, harrumph, there was Joom, right beside my honey tree."

"Joom!" all the others shouted in chorus.

# Toto and the Cats of Oz

Startled by their response, the Bee said in tentative tones, "You know Joom?"

"Sort of," replied the Cowardly Lion.

And Dorothy added, "We suspect him of being involved in the disappearance of my dog, Toto."

"Ha! Well you might, my dear. Well you might," replied the Bee, "for that is just exactly what our argument was about."

"What argument?"

"You know about Toto?"

"Why did you not tell us sooner?"

As the others expressed their surprise, Dorothy just sat there, stunned. Finally, she closed her mouth, opened it again and asked, "What do you know about Toto?"

"I do not really know much, except that Joom holds him prisoner. You can imagine how even one small dog would stand out in a crowd of cats. Oh my, yes, he did! And harrumph, I could not help noticing him. Then when I asked what a dog was doing in this last batch of cats, Joom would only say, 'Oh, he is helping us, too.'

"Well now, I went ahead and put the Counter-Spell on all of them anyway, but my curiosity had the best of me. Yes, indeed. So, herumph, after I was done, in a casual way you know, I flew over to take a closer look. What was my amazement to find the royal seal of Ozma upon his collar! That could mean only the dog from Earth, Toto. And if he was involved, then so was Ozma! And if Ozma, then what need could Joom have of me?

"I can tell you, I was quickly back to that black cat and demanding, harrumph, yes, I was demanding some

76

# The Spelling Bee's Story

answers, but he would not say a thing. Finally he started laughing — a weird and ominous sounding laugh it was, too. Harrumph, yes, ominous! It sent chills up my spine and should have been sufficient to warn me to be suspicious, but it did not. It was not until he spoke to me that I realized what an evil plan he had in mind.

"'You silly old bee' he cackled, 'I have captured Toto to hold him for ransom while I conquer the Emerald City. And you have helped me!'"

"What?" — "Zounds!" — "Impossible!" Several different voices broke in upon the Bee's story simultaneously.

"We cannot let that happen," cried out the Tin Soldier. "Let us march immediately to the rescue!"

"Hold a minute," cautioned the Scarecrow. "Certainly Joom could not overcome the Wizard and all the Emerald City."

"Not with all the cats in Oz!" declared the Tin Woodman.

"I would not be too sure of that," wailed the Spelling Bee. "With my Counter-Spell, there is no way the Wizard's nor Ozma's nor even Glinda's magic can stop them. And, I hear that the Emerald City has no other protection."

"Quite right. It does not," responded the Scarecrow. "And, if magic cannot help us, then we few cannot conquer the cats, either."

"But, at least we know where Toto is now," cried Dorothy with tears running down her cheeks. "He may be a captive, but at least he is safe, and we know where to find him."

# Toto and the Cats of Oz

Responding to her tears, the others gathered around to comfort her and to rejoice with her. Her new tears were soon wiped away and the questioning of the Bee resumed.

"Dids't Joom have his own magic to imprison thee in thine own honey?" asked Sir Hokus.

"Oh no, not magic, just trickery. You see, now he was under the enchantment of the Counter-Spell. Yes, ah yes, that he was. And that Counter-Spell is a kind of magical barrier. Absolutely no magic can pierce it from any direction. I say, not from any direction — neither to help nor to hurt. Harrumph. If you are under the effect of my Counter-spell, no magic can come through it to affect you. No indeed! But then, neither can you send any magic out through it to affect any one else.

"No, it was not magic that Joom used. No, indeed. That avenue was closed to him. All that nasty little rascal needed was his natural dishonesty. You see, when I flew back from discovering that the lone dog amongst the cats was none other than, harrumph, the royal dog Toto, that dastardly Joom was standing right beside my honey tree. That is where he was, right beside my honey tree! As I demanded answers, and he remained quiet, he also casually wandered into the hollow below my honey. Of course, I followed him, still trying to get him to answer my questions.

"Now, on one of his earlier trips, bringing cats to me, he had shown a great deal of interest in how I stored my honey. Oh me! Oh my! That he did! He wanted to know how I made so much, and how I kept it secure in the

# The Spelling Bee's Story

upper part of the tree, and all sorts of things.

"I guess, harrumph, my pride just made me a little simple in the head, because I showed him — Can you believe it? — how I made a huge plug of beeswax and the way I had put three long sticks in to hold it in place.

"You can understand though, can you not, that I might, harrumph, have a bit of justifiable pride in my work. Being so big, I can make more honey and beeswax than a whole hive of ordinary bees."

"I can see that you can make a lot of honey," interrupted the Tiger, "but how did that nasty cat trap you in it?"

"Harrumph, hm, hm. Yes. Well now, you see, while I talked and he remained silent, he had maneuvered so I was at the back of the tree and he was standing in the middle of the hollow. It was then that he finally spoke up and said he was going to conquer the Emerald City."

"Can you imagine his audacity?" demanded the Tin Woodman.

"Even protected against magic," said Dorothy, "it doesn't seem possible."

Holding up his stuffed hand, the Scarecrow warned, "No. But I believe our new friend is correct. Without magic, our dear Emerald City is all too vulnerable."

"Indeed. That is so," agreed the big Bee. "As soon as I heard that spawn of all villainy say he was going to conquer the Emerald City, I knew he could.

"Immediately, I say, *immediately*, I raised my hands and began my incantation of the one spell that will remove the counter-spell. Then, I could have dealt with him on the spot. But I have to give him credit. He was ready for me. Before I could say 'Away and gone,' he lunged at me, and catching me off balance and more than a little startled, harrumph, yes more than a little startled, he was able to push me so that I knocked down the back support. In the same instant, he jumped out the entry hole, taking with him one of the supports beside it, and whoosh, I was covered, caught, trapped in my own dear honey."

At that, everyone let out a sigh, interrupting the Bee's story as they commiserated with him.

When he continued, he told them how the honey was so sticky and weighed him down so that he could not move or do anything to rescue himself. He could not even speak the necessary words with the honey sealing his lips. As he thought of the trouble his careless pride had set afoot he settled to the ground, crying again.

"That's OK. We are here now," said the Tin Woodman as he again placed his metal arm gently across the shoulders of the Bee.

After a few minutes of crying, the giant insect said, "There, I needed that. It makes me feel better. And now you know the whole story."

"Zounds! Now much that was dark is made clear," exclaimed Sir Hokus. "That's why none of our magic could find Toto," said Dorothy, sound almost relieved.

Then Sir Hokus resumed, "On to the Emerald City. Let us smite those cats! I will cut them to the left and to the right."

"Hold on there, Sir Knight," returned the Scarecrow.

# The Spelling Bee's Story

"We cannot do it alone. We need more than we few."

"The Scarecrow is right," added the Tin Soldier. Then, meaningfully, he took out his big sword and, as he wiped it with his oiled cloth, continued, "But, I'm sure we could give a very good account of ourselves, if we had to."

"What are we going to do?" asked the Cowardly Lion.

"We need to raise a big army," replied Captain Fyter. Let me return to the Palace and organize the Winkies."

"And Glinda has her Girl Guards," declared the Hungry Tiger.

"Oh, let's do be careful," returned the Tin Emperor. "We don't really want to hurt anyone if we can possibly avoid it."

"Aw-w," rattled Captain Fyter, "I'd like a good fight, but of course, you're right."

"And," said the Scarecrow, "it may not be as bad as we think. Keeping an army of cats together is going to be no easy task. Cats are pretty independent creatures. The whole thing may well fall apart of its own accord."

"But we can't just sit around waiting!" exclaimed the Hungry Tiger. "We have to try to do something."

"Quite right," answered Dorothy. "I think we ought to hurry to Glinda's. Ozma may still be there, and we can all join in making plans to get Toto back and to stop Joom's revolution."

This was quickly agreed to by all, and as they were remounting, it was decided that, since Jack Pumpkinhead's was on the way, they would stop there for those who needed to sleep.

# Toto and the Cats of Oz

Eventually, the Scarecrow could easily walk all the way to Jack's, for his straw-stuffed body never tired, but that same straw made him a slightly unsteady walker, so he accepted Dorothy's invitation to join her on the Lion's back. Clambering up, he commented, "Now we have more reason for hurrying. It would be tragic if Jack and Button Bright left for the Emerald City before we get there."

They took the path with redoubled effort. For awhile no one said much until Dorothy, speaking to the Spelling Bee with some hesitancy, asked, "Is it possible to remove the Counter-Spell you placed on Toto and the cats?"

Before the Bee could answer, Sir Hokus continued, "If thou canst, then methinks we should have naught to fear of those wayward cats, yea verily."

"Ahem, why yes. Yes, I can. After all nothing can be made fully invulnerable. Yes, indeed. In the strongest armor there is always some fatal chink. So, of course, the Counter-Spell can be removed. Ahem, yes. There is one, and only one way to remove the Counter-Spell. And that, ah yes, that is my secret. Only I know how to place the Counter-Spell and only I know how to remove it.

"So, do not worry. Toto will be all right. Mm-m yes, and I must remove that spell from those dastardly cats as well. You see, of course, ahem, I cannot, I say, I cannot remove or cast any spell unless the subject is within my view. That is right. However indistinct or mumbled my words may be, even if I merely think them while I make the proper motions, ahem, yes, then if I can see it, I can spell it. Yes indeed. And my Dis-Spell will remove any

# The Spelling Bee's Story

spell that has ever been cast. Ahem, umh, yes!"

"Certainly then," exclaimed the Tin Woodman, sounding a bit relieved, "that means there will be no need for fighting."

"Yes," the Scarecrow nodded his head thoughtfully. "As soon as we face Joom and his cats, you can take the Counter-Spell off them and Ozma and Glinda can use their magic to deal with them. Then they will have to return Toto to Dorothy and everyone will be happy once more."

These words were encouraging for all as they rode, now with lighter spirits, across the yellow prairies toward Jack Pumpkinhead's. In Winkieland, of course, the new short wheat growing here was quite yellow. Occasionally there were trees that would wave their yellow branches as the travelers went by.

Discussing their situation further, the Tin Woodman felt that he should go no further than Jack's place. Then, as Emperor of the Winkies, he should bring the news of the cats and what the Spelling Bee could do back to his people and reassure them that everything was under control. The Scarecrow and the Tin Soldier volunteered to stay with him, riding the Hungry Tiger throughout the Winkie Country, spreading the news.

Toward evening, Dorothy was chatting with the Spelling Bee when he asked her, "Do you suppose I should have told our stripped friend that my Anti-hunger spell is one of the short term kind? By morning he will be as hungry as ever."

"No," she whispered. "That will be soon enough for

him to find out."

Dark was coming on, but the two big cats with their night-time vision easily followed the road. Still, it was quite late by the time they all reached Jack's big pumpkin house. There they were all greatly relieved to find the sleepless Pumpkinhead sitting on his front step, whittling.

"My stars and turbans!" he exclaimed. "What are you doing arriving in the middle of the night? Why you must be tired." Unbending his long, thin limbs as he rose to open the door, he continued talking: "And you're all here, my friends, Nick, Dorothy, the Scarecrow, the Cowarr - - -. *What* in the world is that?"

"He is just the largest bee in the world," replied the Tin Woodman, "our new friend, the Spelling Bee. Meet Jack Pumpkinhead, one of our oldest friends."

"Yes," interrupted the Tiger, "and he cast a spell that got rid of my hunger."

"Pleased to meet you, Mr. Bee," said Jack, bowing low in his awkward way. "Won't you come in? All of you?"

As everyone filed into the pumpkin house, Dorothy began telling Jack all about what had happened. Soon everyone was excitedly trying to talk at once, each one filling in some detail he or she thought too important to be left out. Bit by bit the whole story was told. And then, out came Button-Bright, rubbing sleepily at his eyes, awakened by all the noisy chatter. Now everything had to be repeated over again, but it went more quickly the second time through.

When they reached the point of telling about the

# The Spelling Bee's Story

Counter-Spell guarding against all magic, Button-Bright interrupted. "I'll bet that's why none of our magic worked when we tried to find Toto."

"Yes," agreed the Cowardly Lion, "and it probably explains why the pumpkins disappeared from the Magic Picture. Once the cats took the pumpkins, they became as much a part of them as clothing, so of course, the pumpkins disappeared too."

"Quite precisely so. Yes, indeed," agreed the great Bee. "That is exactly the way it would work."

Conversation continued a little longer until the Scarecrow said, "Enough of talk. You who are made of flesh and blood have to get some sleep. We should be off to an early start in the morning. We all have a lot of riding ahead of us."

"Whoopee!" cried Button-Bright. "We ride with the wind to carry word to all the Winkies!"

"I hate to deflate your hopes, little one," said the Tin Woodman, "but since we do have to travel very rapidly, we cannot tire the Tiger by asking him to carry anyone more."

"Aw, but I'm so small. I won't hurt nothin'," he complained.

"No, Button-Bright, I'm afraid that even you would add too much weight," replied the Tin Emperor.

Tears began to form in the little boy's eyes. This made the Woodman worry, for it upset him to see anyone suffer. Although he could think of no solution, the Spelling Bee came to his rescue. First, in his squeaky kind of way, he cleared his throat. Then he commenced: "Now wait a

# Toto and the Cats of Oz

minute here. I think maybe I could be of some help. It may be, yes, I am pretty certain. Harrumph, you see I have a charm that will make you light, all of you. In fact, it should make it possible for you to travel even faster than you did in coming here, because everyone will be so light that the beasts will be easily able to carry all of you. And they, themselves, will practically float along."

"Now, wait a minute," cried the Scarecrow, jumping toward the Bee. "Do I understand correctly that you are getting ready to cast a spell that would make all of us lighter in weight?"

"That is right," responded the Bee.

With his hands resting gently on the Bee's shoulders, the Scarecrow continued, "OK. That is good. But not yet." Then turning to the others with a broad smile, he added, "If he did it now, we might float around the cottage all night."

As everyone laughed, the Bee stammered a little, "Well yes now, ahem. You will not become quite weightless, but then there might be some inconveniences. Yes, we will wait until all are ready to go in the morning."

With this agreed upon, those who needed sleep went off to bed, while the Scarecrow, Jack Pumpkinhead and the two tin men prepared things for the trip.

The next morning, when the people and animals awakened, they found that everything was ready. All they had to do was jump out of bed, dress, eat and go.

As the Hungry Tiger bounded into Jack's main room, he cried out, "Oh, wow! I am hungry again. Hungry. Hungry! Hungry!! It feels normal, so good!" With that he

# The Spelling Bee's Story

waded into a pile of steaks six feet high and did not stop until every one of them was gone.

"Hmmmm. Ver-r-y satisfying," he purred, "but I could take a few more."

While the animals were eating, breakfast was being set out for the humans and the Spelling Bee. Fortunately, he was quite content eating the same food as they, for he was much too big to be able to find enough flower nectar to satisfy him. And what a breakfast it was for all! Did you ever have pumpkin juice, pumpkin soufflé, pumpkin bread toast, fried pumpkin patties, ham slices roasted in pumpkin leaves and pumpkin pie, all for one breakfast?

Of course, the four who had gone without sleeping all night would also go without food all day, for they were not flesh and blood people who had any need for such things. So, while the others ate, these four were busy preparing the Lion and Tiger. Sir Hokus's special saddle was put on the back of the Lion this time, and the baskets of food were strapped to each of the big felines for all those who had need of eating lunch and dinner.

With breakfast over and everyone preparing to leave, the Spelling Bee fluttered up saying, "Ah yes. Now we are ready for my famous Light Spell. Let me see. How does that go? Umh. Yes, I believe I have it now," and, gesturing all four arms toward those that would be riding, he chanted:

"Ramble kabamble, hosh melalao.
Fido, fa faddo, fell and beetauw.

# Toto and the Cats of Oz

Light may it be,
And light it is now."

Instantly, all the would-be travelers began to glow with a bright light, so bright, indeed that the inside of the pumpkin house looked like a sunny summer afternoon. The suddenness of it made the Cowardly Lion cower in a corner, whimpering. Then the voice of the Spelling Bee cut through the surprise.

"Harrumph, umpgh. Let me see here. Well, ah, yes I do, but no, this just will not do at all! But be calm now. Everything is quite all right. I'm afraid that was just the wrong light spell. Ahumph, hum-m."

"Well, it certainly made us all light, all right," laughed Dorothy.

"What wilt thou do now to keep us from shining like torches?" asked Sir Hokus.

"How now, friend knight," asked Jack, "are you afraid that if you were always a light you could not be a knight?"

Ignoring the Pumpkinhead's poor humor, the Bee stammered, "I-I'm so sorry. But do not be afraid. Not at all, for, harrumph, I can use my Dis-Spell to do away with that. Have no fear. You shall soon be your normal, unlit selves." With that, he started waving his arms and antennae in a mystical way while he chanted:

"Away and gone, the spell is wrong.
Let what's been done be now undone."

Just as suddenly as the light had come, it was gone,

# The Spelling Bee's Story

and the room was left in darkness. Jack's own jack-o-lantern lamps still glowed, but the contrast to the brightness was so great that, at first, it seemed as if there was no illumination at all.

"Hmm, now," buzzed the Bee. "What is the right spell? Hmm. Ah yes. Now I have it." And he began to wave an arm.

"Oh! Please wait!" cried out Dorothy. "Are you certain you have the right spell this time?"

"My, yes!" declared the Tin Woodman. "We do not want to add any new problems."

"Ah, my dears," replied the Bee, "have no fears. This is, indeed, the one for lightening loads. Hear now. Listen to the words. Why, even you can lighten some kinds of loads by repeating these words."

Standing quite still, he said:

"Breathe easy, breathe well,
For the load that's big can be small enough.
Only know you've strength to smooth out the rough.
Fret little, fret not,
For the worried load is the heavier load,
And lighter if others can share your road."

In response, the Scarecrow exclaimed, "Sound advice!"

"And that will really make it easy for us to carry everyone, will it?" asked the Lion, timorously.

"Indeed, it will." Then, mumbling half to himself the Bee repeated the lines of his little poem; but this time he wiggled his antennae and moved his four arms, making magic signs in the air as only he could. Even as he spoke, each of the subjects began to feel the new lightness. Indeed, they became so light that Sir Hokus nearly had a catastrophe.

Accustomed to the heaviness of his armor, the knight put his normal energy into jumping into his saddle, and that was enough to propel him clear over the Cowardly Lion. Had he not landed on the back of the Hungry Tiger who was standing a little beyond his chosen steed, his fall to the ground surely would have put a number of dents into his armor.

As for the Scarecrow, by nature already so light, now he could hardly walk without floating around like an air-filled balloon. Each of the travelers experienced his or her own difficulties in adjusting to this new light-weight sensation.

However, before long, all was ready. The two men of metal sat astride the Hungry Tiger with the man of straw between them to keep them from scraping against each other. In front of them, on the Tiger's head sat Button-Bright, and behind them Jack Pumpkinhead clung tightly to the Tin Soldier. They turned and headed north, waving good-bye to Dorothy and Sir Hokus who had already turned toward Glinda's, riding on the Cowardly Lion and accompanied by the flying Spelling Bee.

As they sped along their two paths, little did any of them guess what an exciting turn Dorothy's adventure would take before she and her friends reached Glinda's palace.

# Chapter 10

# Merle Sprekless

Exactly thirty-six days earlier, Merle Sprekless got a job. Jobs were definitely not his thing. He was more into lounging around the waterfront, hitting people up for a dime or a dollar here and there, or generally just taking life easy. But, when he was hungry, a job was better than starving.

Everybody along the waterfront knew him. He was well liked, but he had a hard time adjusting to the things everyone else took for granted. A lot of things he didn't understand, but he was handy. He fixed things that others had trouble with. He opened things that others could not get into. Unfortunately, he could not always tell when it was all right for him to open something and when he should leave it alone, a fact that on occasion got him into trouble.

His best friends were the cats. They didn't worry that he had a hard time understanding. They liked to snuggle up against him for extra warmth when he was sleeping in an alley at night. And it helped to keep him warm, too. He always tried to have some fish with him, or share his food with them. He and the ragged looking black cat, Binkie, were especially good friends.

So, early on a Monday morning, March 14, the two of them were curled up together, sleeping near the foot of a pier at Fisherman's Terminal, across the Canal from Ballard. Hurried steps going right past them woke them slightly and before they could sink back into slumber, a loud voice from the nearby *Sally Mae,* yelled, "What do you mean, 'Lars won't be here?' We can't leave short-handed and we have to leave now!"

An urgent, whispered voice was heard. Then a wiry red-faced man poked his head up from the passageway. "Hey you." Merle looked around and then back at the man, which prompted him to shout, "Yes. You!" Motioning back into the cabin, he said, "He says you can fix things. S'that true?"

Bewildered, Merle shook his head, afraid he was getting into trouble. Then, deciding the Captain meant work and regular eating, he quickly changed it to a rapid nod.

"Well. Which is it? Can you, 'yes,' or can you 'no?'"

Nodding again, Merle stammered, "Uh. Uh. Y-y-e-s. I can."

"Get up here then. I need a mechanic and we're leaving right now!"

Merle turned and scooped up his few belongings in one hand and Binkie in the other.

As he was almost to step on the gunwale of the boat, the Captain commanded, "No cats!"

Merle turned and started to walk away.

"Well, that isn't much of a cat, I guess. We need you more than we don't need him. C'mon!"

# Merle Sprekless

A little fishing boat, way out on the Pacific Ocean, is not a very secure place for a landlubber. Every man in the crew was stronger than he, all knew more about fishing than he ever would, but he understood fixing better than any of them. Out at sea, he was unsteady on his feet, but when they gave him something to fix, he fixed it.

Everything went well until the fifth day out. With no warning, the mighty ocean swells were rushing upon them and soon the winds were harder than they should have been. The little boat was blown this way and that. Water began crashing onto the deck. All the big reels were lost. Portholes broke. The *Sally Mae* was going to pieces, and all Merle could think was, *I can't fix it.*

In the water, he grabbed hold of a fair sized piece of the old boat. He wrapped his arms around it as far as they could go and hung there. Soon he was aware that something kept flopping against one of his arms. It was a piece of rope anchored to the slab. He unwisely twisted around so that the rope held him to the board before he passed out. Had the storm continued, undoubtedly the rope binding him in place would have, at some point, held his head under water long enough to drown him. But the heavy squall was already dying down before he lost consciousness.

Throughout the rest of the day and that night, he passed in and out of awareness. It was not until he could feel sand rubbing against his face and hands as the tide pulled on him that he realized he had washed ashore and was still alive.

He looked around at a wide yellow waste of sand,

# Toto and the Cats of Oz

but beyond it, tree-covered bluffs rose into the sky. There seemed to be no sign of life anywhere. But, shading his eyes, he soon saw a black spot moving a little way down the beach. Should he go toward it or away? It seemed to be moving toward him. Then he heard a feeble "meow," followed by the distant soft words, "Is that you, Merle?"

Maybe he wasn't alive after all. This must be the shores of Heaven, for surely that was Binkie and Binkie had talked in plain ordinary English. Well, being dead wasn't so bad. He was all worn out and hungry, but his best friend was here and they could talk with each other. If this was Heaven and not the other place, they would very soon find some food. He muttered to himself as he hurried toward Binkie, "I guess we'll know pretty soon which place we're in — food or no food."

When they were close to each other, Merle called out, "Did I just hear you talking to me?"

"You sure did. I don't know how come. I've never done that before. But I can now. What's going on?"

"I think we've died and gone to Heaven. Anything can happen there, er, here."

"Hmm. What's Heaven?'

"It's where good people, and I guess animals, go when they die."

"Then, where's the rest of the crew? They were all pretty good people. They made you work, but they fed both of us. None of them ever kicked at me, or you either, for that matter. I got a lot of petting."

It was more thinking than Merle wanted to bother

94

with, so he just muttered "Hmm," and started moving toward the cliffs. Although they looked forbidding out here at low-tide, as they approached closer, it was clear that a number of ravines cutting through would make easy walking. Fresh water was flowing down them and, certainly, that was fruit growing on some of the trees.

They drank and Merle feasted on the produce of the trees. For his part, Binkie slipped out into the brush and soon came back, quite satisfied and licking his lips. They went on up one of the gullies, and soon found the end of it in cliffs and a waterfall. Merle was ready to go back and try another one when, Binkie, poking around, said, "Just a minute. This looks like an old path. It's overgrown now, but I don't think any of these plants are very tough."

Merle decide to try, and in a few minutes found he'd passed beyond the growth and was climbing easily up along side the waterfall.

About half way up they came to a great flat area that stretched beside the towering falls. There was a magnificent view of the ocean. They could see a few islands out in the distance.

Standing, admiring the view, looking up and down the valley and their path, Merle commented, "This wouldn't be a bad place to settle down."

"Plenty of food for you, hunting for me, and water for both of us," said the cat.

"This brush might even make good bedding." Merle was not even thinking about having a roof over his head. It was so seldom that he had ever had one. But, as he examined the brush to see how it would suit for bedding, he could feel a current of air going by him. Then, pushing some of the greenery aside, he could see a large cave behind it. Everything he could see inside it was heavily covered with dust, but the light he let in revealed a large candle, and beside it, a flint lighter.

*Hmmm,* he thought. *Well why not? Doesn't look like anyone uses this place anymore. Might as well see what's here.*

Binkie followed him, muttering "What d'ya know?"

By the lighting of the candle they could see a fairly good sized cave with several passages leading further back. In this first space, there were several hard wooden chairs and small tables. A long and tall cupboard occupied most of the left hand wall while several dusty pictures were hung on the other walls. With no more than a quick glance, they moved on to see what was through the various doorways in the rock.

To the left they found a room with several cupboards of dishes and pans and a little fall of water coming down the far side. It ran through a small sink cut into the rock and on into the next room which Merle discovered could be used as a bathroom.

Returning to the front room and going through the center arch, he found himself in a room with a nice big bed, two wooden chairs, and a couple empty cupboards for hanging clothes. Nothing very interesting, so he went into the last passageway, traveling a little further than either of the other times. Jackpot! There were several tables with nothing but dust on them. Three locked cupboards were around the walls. With a little effort, he knew he could get into them. Against the far wall: two fancy chests — all of leather, with large gold corners, clasps and handles, and bejeweled lettering.

"Treasure, sure, or I'm not Merle Sprekless!"

He was very careful how he went about opening everything. He might not be as smart as some people, but he knew that fine looking chests like these should be handled with care. He could read English just fine, but the labels on these chests and cupboards bore no resemblance to any writing he had ever seen before. However, they certainly were labeled for some purpose.

The first large chest he opened was full of books. That didn't interest him, not at first, anyway. He went to the central, largest cupboard, and worked on the lock for a few minutes until he had it open. It was full of clothes. The style was unfamiliar, but the fit was great. He had never had such fine clothes nor such a good fit. At first, he hesitated, but then he figured that with all the dust around, it certainly looked like all these things had long since been forgotten. Sure. They fit. It was OK for him to wear them.

Back to the smaller chest now. When he finally got it open, he found it packed with many strange items. He puzzled over them for awhile. His fix-it mind kept seeing relationships between them. This one should fit on this one. This one should be able to wind this one. You can pump with this one. Certain ones fit into others for grinding purposes. There were many envelopes and vials of powders and some bottles of liquids. All of these were labeled, again with that strange script.

# Toto and the Cats of Oz

He turned back to the box of books. Yes, some of them had pictures that looked like some of the equipment. Again, he couldn't read anything, but it gave him the feel of something magical.

One of the implements looked like a magic wand to him, so he tried making up commands as he waved it. Nothing happened.

He studied some of the picture series, and judged that he was beginning to understand how one or two devices might work magic. But he wasn't sure. The problem kept vexing him and he kept working at it. Hours went by. Finally, in the middle of the night, although deep in the caverns he knew not whether it was day or night, he sought out the bed and went to sleep.

It was not a good sleep. He kept having terrible nightmares, being attacked by the magical implements, by the waves, by the ship, by another man, by giant cats. He kept trying to get away from one or the other and never could. Often, in his sleep, he would cry out, "Leave me alone. Let me be."

Binkie was concerned about the terror in his friend's voice and tried to wake him up, but nothing availed. Finally, Merle quieted down, and both of them slept.

The cat was up long before the man, out getting his breakfast, and investigating his new surroundings. In mid-morning he settled down on the wide platform of rock outside the cave door and napped.

At last the man came out, too. Binkie took one look, then a sniff and jumped back, his hair standing straight on end. This was not Merle. Gone were the familiar odors of inquisitiveness and comfortable satisfaction. Here were angry, fearful odors. This man was the same size as his old friend, but his face was long, contorted and deeply lined, his ears were large and round, he seemed to wear a perpetual frown and he had two straps around his body.

Saying nothing, Binkie ran past him into the shelter of the caves, straight to the bedroom, but there was no Merle. He sniffed at the bedclothes and could detect the smell of both men, so thought his hobo friend must still be around someplace. He investigated everywhere, but could find no trace of him.

Outside, he found the stranger sitting on the edge of the cliff, looking out to the sea and humming a mournful tune.

The cat demanded, "What did you do with Merle?"

"Oh, don't worry, Binkie," answered the strange man. "I haven't hurt him in the least. He may be back again when it's time."

"What do you mean, 'may be?'"

The other tried to smile, but it looked more like a sneer. "Not to worry. My name is 'Joom.' Merle is quite safe. No harm will come to him." With that he walked back inside and started busying himself with the same implements Merle had been so interested in the night before. Binkie did not exactly trust what the other had said, but decided to stick around awhile and see what happened. So it went for the next several days.

Early Friday morning, Joom, leaning on his staff and trying to sound quite gentle, called the cat to him. Binkie poked his head out of the bushes, but still stayed several feet from the strange man. He sat down on his haunches, asking, "Well? What do you want?"

"My dear Binkie, it bothers me that you are so mistrustful of me. We should be very close to each other." He took a step closer. The cat jumped up on all fours, ready to run as Joom leaned again on his staff, continuing to speak. "Actually, I have thought that maybe we could reunite you and Merle. He is quite safe, but he misses you, and wishes the two of you could be together again. Would you like that?"

The black cat started circling the man, staring hard at him. "I don't trust you. How can you get us together again?"

Turning so he could keep looking at the cat, Joom answered, "I'm the one that sent him, ah, on a little errand for me. He is doing just fine where he is, but I think it would be wise to send you to be with him. That's all."

Unfortunately, curiosity was getting the best of the cat, and before he could react, Joom's long staff had touched him and he had disappeared, but he had been replaced by an old black jug.

"Ah, ha, ha! Thought you could avoid me, did you?" And sweeping the jug under one arm, he strode into his Room of Magic, where he placed it on a handy shelf and busily began mixing powders, liquids and ointments, humming off-tune as he did.

In a few minutes time, stinking fumes were being generated by his work, but he seemed oblivious to them. Then he smeared the jug with the mess he had prepared, tapped it quickly with his rod, and there stood the cat, alive, but quite immobile. This gave the magician plenty of time to stamp each foot three times while leaning on his rod and clearly enunciating between each pair of stamps, "Unite us. Unite us. Unite us." In a small flash of light, Binkie was gone.

Twirling around, Joom shouted, "I've got it! I've got it! Everything is working. Wow! We're all three together."

Then picking up his rod again, he mumbled, "Now for the next step. Ha, ha, ha." This time between pairs of stamps, he was saying, "Binkie, Binkie, Binkie," and he was gone to be replaced by Binkie.

The cat laughed, but it sounded just like the same crazy laugh the man had just used. "I've got it! They'll never know it is me until it is too late. I can be a cat, and I can rule the cats! Ah, ha, ha, ha!"

Crazily he whirled around the room, then out into the other rooms. He jumped on the furniture, high onto the bureau, ran outside and rushed up the closest tree, laughing wildly the whole time.

Finally, he settled down, went back to his Room of Magic, jumped onto a table and lapped up all the liquid he had left there in a saucer. Making a sour face at it, he jumped softly from the table, took a firm grip on the strap he had used earlier, and said, "I want to be in the woods just north of the Emerald City of Oz."

He was gone from the cave, and in the woods just north of the Emerald City, there was a mysterious scraggly looking black cat with two straps around his body and that long rod stuffed through them. In three weeks Dorothy would discover that Toto was missing.

# Chapter 11

## Into the Chambers of Magic

hen Ozma, Uncle Henry, Scraps and the Sawhorse arrived at the Ruby Castle, Glinda rushed them immediately into the special room where she kept her Magic Record Book. That marvelous volume automatically records every significant event in Oz and the surrounding magical countries just as it happens.

As they hurried along, she said, "Thank heavens you are here! I could not believe my eyes and thought that possibly all was lost. It is simply unbelievable and tragic."

Mystified, the others ran along the hall behind her and when they reached the room, she pointed at the open book, saying, "That is what I was reading just as you were announced!"

There, before their eyes, were the words, "The Emerald City has fallen and all its inhabitants taken captive."

Uncle Henry let out a low whistle as Ozma said, "How can that be?"

Scraps, for the second time in a day, was speechless.

"You can see why I was both surprised and happy to

see you just now," said the red-haired Glinda.

"This is terrible!" exclaimed Ozma. "Does it not say anything about who made this conquest?"

"Not one word. This is absolutely the first and only reference to it," replied Glinda.

"Someone has a mighty powerful magic if he can sneak up on the Emerald City thataway and still keep his name out o' your Magic Book of Records," remarked Uncle Henry.

"I'm afraid you're right," replied the Sorceress. Then turning to Ozma, she asked, "Who did you leave in charge when you left."

"The Wizard," was the little Queen's brief reply.

"I was afraid of that," continued the Good Witch, as she slowly shook her head. "Then, it would also take a great deal of magic to overcome him."

"And now our unknown enemy has all of the Wizard's magic equipment as well as mine." Ozma's voice sounded quite troubled, and Glinda began pacing up and down the room, showing an unaccustomed nervousness.

"He could be watching us right now," complained the Sawhorse.

"Aw, but then none of that equipment is working anyway," laughed Scraps, trying rather unconvincingly to sound lighthearted.

"No. Everything seemed to work fine so long as we were not trying to find Toto," said Ozma. "For some reason, someone was just keeping him as a hidden secret."

"That was probably part of his plan for capturing the

Emerald City," interjected Glinda from the far end of the room.

"But what can Toto have to do with the Emerald City being captured?" Uncle Henry wondered aloud as he, too, began to pace.

For a few minutes all was silent save for the click of Glinda's high heels and the clomp of Henry's big boots. It was Ozma who finally broke the silence, saying, "Glinda, the Wizard and I were concerned about a cat that appeared in the Emerald City about two weeks ago. His name is Joom, and we think he is some sort of a magical cat."

"Yes," added Uncle Henry as he stopped his pacing, "it seems like he might be responsible for all this."

"Do you think there is any way you could find out more about him?" asked Ozma.

"I believe I could, but I will need your help, Ozma. First," she clapped her hands for a guard, "Permina will have the house staff help the rest of you to your rooms. Let us be on our way."

Going down the hall, away from the others, Glinda said to Ozma, "Before checking on Joom, there is something else we must do. We must go to my Chambers of Magic, a place I should have introduced you to long ago."

This was a shock even to Ozma, for the rooms the Red Sorceress referred to were rooms of rumor. It was said that someplace in the castle were chambers so bound by magical charms that no one but Glinda could find them. In these rooms it was supposed that the highest

# Into the Chambers of Magic

kind of magic was performed. Here she had fashioned her Great Book of Records. Here she had cast the Magic Picture for Ozma. Here the greatest of all magic could be performed.

She never took anyone else into these secret rooms. Not even Ozma had ever been there before. Now they went together through many halls and corridors, heading for the very center of the palace. On the way they came to a group of Glinda's red-clad girl guards.

"Teriane," said the Sorceress, speaking to one of the girls wearing the Captain of the Guard's sleeve decorations, "see to it that a double guard is put upon the walls from now on. They should be equipped with gloom-piercing lights to see into the night or any other darkness."

"Is there trouble?" asked the pert little black-haired girl to whom Glinda had spoken.

"Yes, and it may be the worst we have ever seen. The Emerald City has already fallen. So I also want you to send scouts out to keep a constant watch in the woods. Provide them with some of the Wizard's disappearing pills, just in case."

"I will do so immediately, but what should we be looking for?" asked the girl.

"That is just the trouble," replied Glinda. "We do not know."

As Teriane sped upon her duties, Glinda continued on, leading Ozma up to the third floor. Here they came to Glinda's Magic Workroom, where common magic was performed. A large key gave her ingress. Several tomes of magic lay upon the tables, and a few pieces of magical looking equipment were set up about the room. Several shelves held a variety of bottles, boxes and tubes, but Glinda ignored all this and walked straight across the room, pausing between the windows in front of a solid enough looking wall. She quickly touched various of the stones in succession, while muttering a few words that Ozma could hardly hear. The surfaces of the rocks separated, revealing a winding staircase reaching into the depths of the castle.

As they descended the stone steps, Ozma said, "I never believed the talk that you had anything more magical than the room we just left."

"Long ago I set up this center surrounded by such powerful charms that no form of magic can penetrate them — not even your Magic Picture. Even you, my dear friend and ruler could not get down here without my help."

The two fell silent as they continued down the staircase. Reaching the bottom brought them to a short but dank and echoing tunnel, at the end of which Glinda moved aside a creaking door and they entered a room clothed in a darksome mood. Only stray bits of light seemed to filter through the room. Heavy, dark drapes hung here and there upon the walls, frequently separated by great wooden bookcases. A few dusty, musty old volumes were upon them, but mostly they were covered with jars full of strange and magical oddments — bat's wings, vulture's tongues, witch's hair and the like. A skull sat upon a table and one glass-fronted cupboard had various selections of bones. Cobwebs were in

# Into the Chambers of Magic

abundance.

"Ooo," shuddered Ozma.

"What is it," asked Glinda.

"Well, it's hard to say, but I did not expect your most private Chamber of Magic to be so sinister. It seems to be a remainder from the worst days of magic."

"Not a remainder, dear Ozma, but a reminder! A reminder of the horrible results our magical arts can produce when wrongly used. This is not a work room, only a museum and a kind of portal. I shiver too when I come though here."

They had taken only a few steps into the room by this time but two great black ravens suddenly flew down toward them out of the darkness above. A startled little cry escaped Ozma's lips, but she quickly regained her composure as they settled upon the back of a chair beside her.

Alternating stanzas, they croaked:

"Puss is gone,
Fled the chamber."

"Since the dawn,
Have not seen her."

"Think upon
Why she'd wander."

"Like a pawn
Of other power."

# Toto and the Cats of Oz

Shrinking away from them, Ozma asked, "What do they mean?"

"I am not quite certain. There should be a big black cat in here too, but they say she is gone, and they think that some other magician may be responsible. But, I cannot see how that could happen."

"Oh-h, Oh," declared Ozma. "I am afraid there might be a connection between this and Joom and the disappearance of Toto. Could it be that someone is already at work in your palace, too?"

Again, the birds spoke in alternation:

"No one here has come.
Puss went out alone.

"You may strike us dumb,
Make us only moan,

"Send us out to bum,
Should you in this zone

"Find that strangers come
Past your magic bone."

Looking across the room, Ozma could see the giant bone they indicated glowing a soft yellowish-white and hanging upon the far wall.

"That is all right, my dread ravens. I believe you. Your words are always true." So saying, Glinda pushed aside a heavy drape near the glowing bone and ushered

# Into the Chambers of Magic

Ozma through the low arch it hid and into another short passageway. As the curtain dropped behind them, she continued, "Those birds! Not only do they always speak the truth, but they know as well as I that the bone would glow a ruby red if any intruder even approached these rooms, or if anyone should try to work magic in my palace or any place near it without my permission."

Ozma shivered a little as she replied, "They may speak truly, but 'Dread Ravens' is surely the right name for them. I'd have been scared without you."

"Oh, they're harmless enough," laughed Glinda. "Really, they are quite friendly. Their names and the way they act are just a part of the effect I want in my Chamber of Darkness. But come, here we are at the entrance to the Chamber of Light, the font of all my magic."

Opening the door, they stepped into a room that seemed to be in sunlight. Yet, as she looked around, Ozma could see no windows anywhere. It was not sunlight. It just looked like it, radiating warmly, yellowish, throughout the room. The darkness of the first room was gone, to be replaced by the light and color of this room. As there had been a lonely emptiness about the cluttered heights of the Chamber of Darkness; so, in the low-ceilinged Chamber of Light, there was a feeling of coziness and warmth.

Glinda waved her hand and the light was restricted to a glow outlining every object in the room. Another flourish of her hand and there was just one, intensely bright beam shining right down on the center of the room. As Glinda slowly circled her hand around, the

109

beam traced the same circle out in the room. Then with a clap of her hands, the chamber was once more bathed in light, but this time it was a reddish light.

Watching this amazing display, Ozma had noticed one globe sitting on a stand by the far wall. Throughout all the changes in lighting effects, it had remained the same soft, yellowish-white glow just like the bone in the Chamber of Darkness. As Glinda restored the appearance of daylight, Ozma asked her about the glowing orb.

The Sorceress answered: "In each of these rooms of magic there is something that glows red to warn me of the presence of any unexpected magic or magic workers."

"What a wondrous system this is!" declared the little Queen. "It must have taken a lot of work to develop it."

"Yes. My early protection was not enough. Remember, long ago when all our best magic was stolen, all at the same time? That was it for me. I decided I had to have real security and some sort of permanent warning procedure for my real rooms of magic. It took a long time to work out the necessary charms, but about forty years ago I had developed them and quietly began hollowing out this space. You can see the results."

"Have these ever been called upon to give you warning?"

"Not yet," replied the Good Witch, "and I had hoped that time would never come."

"You always have new ways to amaze me," exclaimed Ozma. "Only one thing bothers me about this one. You

# Into the Chambers of Magic

do not spend a lot of time down here. What if someone tries magic when you are someplace else in the castle?"

"As a matter of fact, I count on these glowing instruments as our first line of defense. If a strange worker of magic should even come as close as the woods and plains surrounding this castle, these devices will immediately begin to glow very lightly, getting more intense as the intruder comes closer. Then Puss and the Dread Ravens have their own secret ways to come tell me."

"And," asked the Queen, "are we any better prepared to meet it here than we were in the Emerald City?"

"Not yet," responded the Red Witch, "but we will be. That is why we came down here. As I said, no one can enter these rooms unbidden, but similar permanent protection for the whole palace would be impractical. However, for awhile I have been working on a plan for emergency protection and that emergency seems to be here now. It will take a while for me to set it up."

"Us?"

"Yes, 'Us,' I will need you to help me, both in arranging these devices and in preparing the Enchantment of Protection."

With that, Glinda began pulling things out of drawers and cupboards. Before long, she seemed to have everything ready.

"All right now," she said. "We are ready."

The first thing they did under Glinda's instruction was to begin placing certain little posts at intervals. Next they sprinkled a kind of reddish gravel in lines between them. Other posts with mystic symbols, and other colors of gravel, beads and sand were also spread about. Finally the sorceress had only three large packets of powder left. One she gave to Ozma, and two she kept for herself.

Moving to the wall, the Red Witch opened a cupboard, revealing an array of dials, knobs, buttons and levers. She pushed several of the buttons and twisted a few knobs. A buzzing sound began. Then she pulled on a big red lever, and the knob beside it began to glow green. Slowly, Glinda turned that knob. As she did, Ozma was amazed to see that a brilliant light was emanating from the very center of the room. As the light extended out from itself, growing brighter all the time, the walls of the room grew dimmer. Gradually, in their place, the battlements surrounding the palace became visible.

"Now, Ozma," said Glinda, "follow me along these shadow walls. Scatter the powder I gave you and move your wand in the same way I move my Sorcerer's Rod, saying, as the grains settle to the ground, 'Gettle, gettle, bey ma deddle.' Keep repeating that all the way around until we return to this same spot."

With those words, Glinda opened one of her packets of powder and began sprinkling it along the ethereal palace walls. Ozma followed behind her doing just as she had been instructed. When they finished their circuit of the walls, Glinda took the last packet of powder and led Ozma to the center of the room.

"Here," she said, "stand facing me. Do not do a thing except to mimic my actions, and do not say a word except to repeat my phrases. You might be startled by

# Into the Chambers of Magic

some of the things that happen, but I know you will take them in stride."

Then Glinda opened her remaining packet and poured the powder in it over both of them. As she did so, Ozma could see that their garments began to glow. The Good Witch remained standing perfectly still, as in a trance, so Ozma did too. Finally the glow began to fade. And in the fading, Glinda's red gown and Ozma's green one both turned to ashen gray. Now Ozma could see that Glinda's face and hands were taking on a red luster. With the slightest glance at her own hands, she saw a green sheen coming upon them.

Unbelievable! Here her friend was mixing red magic with green magic, a thing usually resulting in catastrophe. The very thought made a sweat break out on Ozma's brow and she came close to trembling. What impossibly great power was being used to accomplish this! It gave her an eerie feeling, only reinforced as the young Queen realized that she was copying Glinda's every movement in perfect unison without even thinking about it. An observer would not be able to tell who was copying whom.

Effortlessly now, both of them sat upon the floor. Looking down, they passed their hands back and forth, each over the others, a few inches from the floor and began to chant:

Whoosh and swoosh, oh great round wind
Whose only way is through these walls,
Within this room and 'round it, wail.

# Toto and the Cats of Oz

Again and again they repeated this incantation. Louder and louder became their words. As they continued to chant, Glinda began to turn, slowly at first, then faster and faster. Ozma found herself unconsciously doing the same. As they turned, they gradually rose again to an upright position. In the process, Glinda was growing larger, and in one corner of her mind, Ozma realized that she was doing likewise. Their robes swirled around them in great billows. Sure enough, a wind was now howling through the room. Ozma could hear it, and she could see the powders blowing in great draughts and gusts, but not a hair on her head was disturbed, nor could she feel the least movement of the air.

As Glinda reached a full standing position, the red began to return to her robes and her face and hands took on their natural color once more. The howl of the wind came to a crescendo and then stopped. In the silence, both girls' voices were soft but firm:

"Fly, oh winds. With every breeze
Protect us from all mysteries."

Immediately the wind roared again, even louder than before. There was a great flash of light, and then darkness. When the howl of the wind died down, the light began to return. Ozma could see that the room was just as it had been before. All was quiet. They had each returned to their normal size, and there were no signs of powders, potions, posts, or ethereal battlements.

# Into the Chambers of Magic

Glinda nodded her head and in an exhausted tone said, "It is done."

"Whewie!" exclaimed the young Queen. "What a display! I have seen some pretty good ones. In fact I have put on a few myself. But that beats all."

"I should hope so," returned Glinda. "That was the point of it — 'to beat all' — any combination, magical or otherwise that the mysterious magician might bring against us."

"We are safe then?"

"I do not know," replied the Witch of the South. "It is the strongest defense I have, but after all the strange things that have happened, I just do not know if even this is enough."

# Chapter 12

# A Misadventure on the Road

agic completed, the two young ladies mounted the stairway back into the beautiful Ruby Palace. Although it was now late at night, they headed for the little kitchen on the first floor, hoping to find something to take the place of dinner. What was their surprise, as they passed the throne room, to find the doors open, the lights on, and a hubbub of voices within. Most of the residents of the castle were there, and they were all gathered around the Wizard, the Shaggy Man and Tik-Tok.

As soon as they appeared in the doorway, the voices stopped, motion ceased, and all eyes turned toward them. The irrepressible Scraps was the first to move. Bounding across the room, she cried out, "What's the news?"

"We have placed the most powerful protection that magic can provide around this palace," replied Glinda. Then she told them a little about the purpose of the magic that she and Ozma had prepared. But this time, feeling it would be best to have her people feeling strong and confident, she voiced no doubts.

# A Misadventure on the Road

Teriane reported that she had placed guards and scouts as directed and after a little more talking, everyone went on to the dining hall. At last, Glinda and Ozma could have dinner—a real one. And, it so happened that in their anxiety most of the others had not had much to eat themselves, so a grand meal was shared by all.

The next morning Glinda and Ozma returned to the Chambers of Magic to study its records. They dug into every clue they could, but nothing showed up until late in the day when Ozma stood up, her finger on a particular spot in the volume she was perusing, and shouted, "This might be it!"

Glinda swung around to stand by Ozma where she could see for herself: "The illegal transformation of Prince Bobo of Boboland was accomplished in the Year 1383 Of Oz by an unnamed magician. Soon after that, the cruel magician disappeared, never to be heard from again, and it has long been presumed that someone succeeded in destroying him. Recent research has shown that the perpetrator of that transformation was the renegade, Joom. Until the Wizard of Oz saw through the enchantment in 1512 O.Z., no one knew what had become of the dearly loved Bobo. At that time, Glinda the Good of Oz restored Bobo to himself and his country."

"So!" exclaimed the Good Witch, "Much is revealed." Then as, out of curiosity, she turned the book over, she added, "What do you know? Bragwost's *History of Eastern Ozia*. I just got this from across the Desert last month."

"So," observed Ozma, "it appears that Joom was not

# Toto and the Cats of Oz

destroyed, has been in hiding and has now returned."

"Precisely, and that is not good. Little was known of that unnamed magician, except that he was very wicked, resourceful and a master of transformations. Yes, probably at last, and to our discomfort, he has resurfaced.

"But, come now. We have earned our dinner and it is almost that time."

When they rejoined the others, there was a great deal of excitement over their discovery. Everyone felt a bit more settled, ready to proceed to the next phase. While they ate, it was decided that all the good magic workers they could find would be needed to combat the menace of Joom. His powers had been strong enough to overcome the Wizard and defy the Magic Picture, the Magic Belt and the Magic Book of Records. Glinda would summon several of her friends directly through magic. She would also send two of her guards in her stork-drawn chariot to recruit friends from across the Deadly Desert. Ozma, Scraps and Uncle Henry would take the Sawhorse and the Red Wagon to gather several others from the north.

"Maybe we'll find more help up there than we are expecting," remarked Ozma, but she said no more about it.

Once they had their plans settled, Glinda insisted, "It is very late now and we all need to be well rested for what lies ahead of us."

"You're right," agreed Uncle Henry. "There'll be time enough for rushin' 'round after a good night's sleep."

118

# A Misadventure on the Road

"I never need to sleep, so I'll get food and stuff packed while the rest of you get your beauty rest," laughed Scraps.

With that, "Good nights" were said and all the others went off to bed.

By mid-morning all were up and breakfast was over. Two of the guards took off in the stork cart, circled once, and headed out to the northeast to go beyond the Deadly Desert. Ozma, Scraps, and Uncle Henry got into the Red Wagon at the front gates of the palace, and with Glinda and many of her Girl Guards waving them on, set out upon their mission. The direct route would lead them through the Emerald City, so they had decided to detour a little to the east.

Pausing at the top of the surrounding hills, Ozma and her friends looked back to drink in the beauty of the lush red valley they were leaving.

Although all the Land of Oz has been blessed with a mild, warm climate, only in this broad basin was there found the true California-type climate with the vibrant, clean, dry heat of the blossoming desert. Indeed, in the time of the Wicked Witches, the dryness of the desert had extended to within a mile of the Castle. Over the years since, Glinda and her Quadling farmers had reclaimed many miles of sandy waste and made it bloom luxuriously. The streams flowing down from the Mountains of the Hammerheads and the nearby Roseate Hills and Red Mountains had provided water which the workers had channeled to where it was needed for crops and gardens. Now, this fertile land of the Ruby

119

# Toto and the Cats of Oz

Vale produced an abundance of flowers, fruit, vegetables and grains. Sitting in the middle of this glowing valley, Glinda's Castle, indeed, sparkled like a carved giant red ruby.

They had time for only a brief, but lingering look at the beautiful setting. Then the four plunged on into the red forest, skirting the Hammerhead Mountains lying to their west, and heading toward the mountain where Dr. Pipt lived. It stood just barely outside the Quadling Country, in the Land of the Munchkins. Had they reached their destination, they were to have recruited that famous Crooked Magician. However, when the road broke out into a wide prairie of tall red grass waving in the breeze, they found their way blocked by a group of cats. When these saw our travelers, they all sat right down in the middle of the road and the Sawhorse had to stop to keep from hitting them.

"Hey! Out of the road!" demanded the Sawhorse in his usual rough tones. "Can't you see we are in a hurry?"

"You're in no hurry," answered one of the cats. "You're under arrest."

With an angry glare in his wooden eyes, the Sawhorse reared a little and started saying, "Now, look here, Tabby …" but Uncle Henry interrupted in calmer tones:

"I think there must be some mistake. This is Ozma, the Ruler of all the Land of Oz."

"Sure, Buddy. We know she's Ozma, for all we care, but she ain't the ruler of any part of the Land of Oz! Not anymore! Come along, now, before we get mean!"

With that, all the cats arched their backs and hissed

# A Misadventure on the Road

a little.

"It's all right." Ozma spoke reassuringly to her friends, "We will go along with them."

Threateningly, the cuts muttered, "You'd better."

The Sawhorse grumbled, but obedient to Ozma, he started up again, this time, following the cats. More of them had come out of the long grass and the horse cart was now totally surrounded by felines of all sizes and colors. They were lead off to the west, across the prairie to a little used wagon track leading through the woods back to the main road between Glinda's Castle and the Emerald City.

The trip through the woods was uneventful. The cats continued to heckle the travelers. The Sawhorse tended to take affront, but Ozma kept reassuring him that the feline taunts were not worthy of a response, "If we remain quiet, they will eventually give up. But the more angrily we react against their remarks, the more we will encourage them to keep at it."

After reaching the north-bound road, they followed it for some way toward the Emerald City. So long did they go that Scraps started getting a little anxious and, leaning close to Ozma, whispered, "It's time we were getting about our business. Why don't you turn them to stone or something so that we can?"

As the other two occupants of the carriage leaned closer to hear, Ozma responded, "That is exactly what I have been trying to do ever since this started, but nothing works."

"What'aya mean?" gasped Uncle Henry.

121

# Toto and the Cats of Oz

"By this time they should be stones or caterpillars or bushes, or we should have walked right past them while they stood still, unable to touch us. But we are still here and they are still there."

"Still? I should say not," responded the Patchwork Girl with a silly giggle. "I'd say we were all moving along at a right smart pace. They are not very still and neither are we."

Chuckling at Scraps patchy sense of humor, Uncle Henry asked, "Seriously, what is happening? Are you losing your magical powers?"

"I don't know what to make of it," replied Ozma. "Just to check, I have turned rocks to pieces of wood, and once I turned a butterfly into a bird and back again. But nothing I have tried on the cats has had the least affect."

They were already moving from the red fields of Quadlingland into those green grasses that extend widely around the Capital City. The occupants of the cart were getting a bit on edge. If they were going to escape, it would have to be soon.

Ozma said, "All we need is a little diversion."

"Good enough. I'll see what I can do," and Scraps leaned precariously out of the cart, practically dragging her head in the dust of the road as she called out, "What's been going on in the Emerald City since we left?"

"Hah! You'd be surprised!" exclaimed one cat.

"We're having a great time," said another. "We've taken over and everything's going our way."

Then a third joined in, "Sure. The people are serving

122

# A Misadventure on the Road

us now."

"We come and go when we please, and we eat what we please. No more meowing to get in and out. No more just eating what you give us. No more passively following your rules." A big gray cat was speaking now. "We've got it just the way we want it for a change."

"No more running to "Kitty, kitty, kitty,'" said yet another.

A sixth cat laughed, "Yeah, now we call, "Person, person, person,' an' ya should see 'em scamper! We've got sharp claws!" With that he let out a hiss and took a swipe at Scraps who was still leaning low over the side of the carriage. One claw caught her face near the left ear, making a long rip down to her chin. The exposed cotton began bulging out the slit as Ozma dragged her back into the carriage amidst a chorus of laughs and cat calls.

"Ha," said one, "Joom has sure turned the tables on you, little Miss Ozma. And he has Toto, too."

"So! Joom is behind all this!" she exclaimed.

"Not behind it," answered another cat. "He is the head of it. He is the King Cat of all Oz, and you people ain't nothin' at all anymore."

"Except that you can be our pets if you behave yourselves," said another.

Yet one more chimed in with, "You're no queen of nothin' at all from now on, an' your magic can't harm us. Ha, ha," and all the cats began laughing again.

This was the chance Ozma wanted. She whispered softly to the Sawhorse. He responded with a loud snort and by racing off to the right, kicking his gold-shod heels out wildly as he went. The cats scattered before this sudden outburst of energy, and horse, carriage and riders took off right across the green fields to the east. Immediately all the 120 or so cats gave chase. It was no match. The Wooden Sawhorse's boundless energy enabled him to travel like the wind and the cats were soon left far behind.

However, it was not long before the horse discovered that he was in trouble. Bushes had begun to dot the meadows, and as he proceeded, now beginning to climb into the mountains that formed the border between the lands of the Quadlings and of the Emerald City, there was less of grass and more of brush until he was considerably slowed, twisting this way and that through the growing thickets. Finally he reached a place where no route was open and the carriage became fast stuck in the tangle.

Maybe the tear in her face had effected the Patchwork Girl's usually cheerful disposition, for she moaned, "Now what will we do?"

"Someone unhitch me. That is what we can do! I can carry you as easily on my back as in the carriage." There was a slight sound of exasperation in the voice of the Sawhorse, as though he thought someone should have done that without needing to be reminded by him.

Uncle Henry jumped down and unfastened the harness from the wagon tree as the others climbed out of the carriage and onto the back of their worthy wooden steed.

"Watch how fast you go," warned Ozma. "I have had

# A Misadventure on the Road

experience with you, and I know how badly a person's bones can be jolted."

Even in distress, a little of the Patchwork Girl's spirit seemed to revive as she added,

"Most certainly watch how you're trottin',
I don't want to loose any cotton.
This gash in my face
Is quite a disgrace.
Now, how could a cat be so rotten?"

Uncle Henry had been busily making reins out of the harness, and handing them to Ozma, said, "Here then. That will give you something to hang on to. I will sit at the back and Scraps can sit between us, with each of us hanging on to the one in front of us."

As they took their places, the girl Ruler said, "I hate to leave the carriage behind, but it has slowed us down to the point that I'm sure the cats have begun to gain on us."

"An' they couldn't have missed the trail that buggy was beating through the brush," added Uncle Henry.

"Now maybe we can really lose them," exulted Scraps.

"Yes," and Ozma spoke to the Sawhorse next, "Turn strongly to the northeast here. Going through these hills, deeper into the Emerald City territory, we will soon come to a more rocky ground. That will be a good place to go where I intend — off to the southeast. By that time those cats will certainly have lost all track of us."

# Toto and the Cats of Oz

Off then, they sped. For awhile, with the roughness of their way, and the horse racing at such a speed, turning and twisting through trees and brush, no one could say anything. As a matter of fact, for about fifteen minutes, everyone was so busy hanging on tight and watching the ground right in front of them that no one really noticed that the hills were turning into mountains.

Finally, Ozma nudged the Sawhorse, gasping, "All right. All right, now," and he slowed down until she could clearly say, "This is about it. Off we go up the mountain to the right."

As the wooden animal turned, and before he could get up to speed again, Uncle Henry called out, "Imagine we've pretty well lost them cats by now. Maybe there's no call t' go quite so lickity-split anymore."

"Indeed, Henry," responded the Queen, and then to the Sawhorse, "He's right, we really don't have to hurry any longer, my old friend. We seem to be safe and near our goal."

So he slowed his pace even further, and the riders could finally talk again and enjoy the mountain scenery that now surrounded them.

Uncle Henry was saying, "It's a caution what we find way off the beaten path this-a way — beautiful big mountains and now the snow is beginning to show."

"You're right," rejoined the Patchwork Girl. "Since we don't have a lot of high mountains in Oz, I'm beginning to wonder if we're getting close to Christmas Valley."

"I'll bet that was yer intention th' whole time!" exclaimed Uncle Henry. "I just heard you say we're 'near

126

# A Misadventure on the Road

our goal,' Eh Ozma?"

The Queen laughed, "I admit it. After we left Glinda's, I began thinking it might be a good idea to check with Santa Claus."

"Of course," Scraps commented, "he knows all about every one in the world. So he might know something more about this Joom."

"An' the way the cats led us, we'd a been up a creek if we'd tried to go any way but this here one," added Uncle Henry.

"Heigh-ho!" shouted Scraps. "It's off we go over the snow to Santa Claus's Workshop!"

# Chapter 13

# The Fall of the Emerald City

xciting things were happening everywhere and the Emerald City had not been left out. On the day the search parties had set out to look for Toto, everything had seemed peaceful enough in the capital. Everyone waved good-bye to the various groups and cheered them on as they left. Then the citizens of the city returned to their usual activities. Not the least of these was the Guardian of the Gate, who, first pushed the great golden latticework that adorned the entrance to the Emerald City back into place, and then turned to one of his usual activities—checkers.

When the Wizard ruled Oz, he had built the Emerald City, not only as his capital, but also as a defensive position out of fear of the Wicked Witches. So he had the walls built sturdy and strong and with only one way through them. Instead of a great city gate, there was just a door in the wall. For a door it was both big and heavy and it led into the Guardian's Room. Across the room, a similar door led through the wall and into the city. The Wizard not only wanted protection from the evil witches, but he also wanted to discourage all visitors.

# The Fall of the Emerald City

When Ozma became Queen, she still wanted to provide protection for her people, yet she also wanted to make the walls an invitation to friends and visitors. Therefore, she had the walls beautified and she had four great gateways cut into them. The harsh, straight lines of the top of the wall she had modified by lovely towers placed along it ever so often, with crenellated battlements stretching in between. The gates seemed to be made of rods of gold, twisted and turned into fanciful designs. In reality, they were quite solid. Entwined bars of gold could easily be bent and broken and would hardly deter any invader. Ozma had used her fairy magic to create a magical illusion of light and beauty. This same magic made it possible to look right through what were, in reality, very solid gates.

Now, as the crowds returned to homes, shops, schools and play, Faramant, the Guardian of the Gates, invited his good friend, Omby Amby, to join him in a few games of checkers. For an hour or more, they played quite steadily. Neither saying much more than, "Your move," or "King me."

Finally, after each of them had won four games, the bewhiskered soldier commented, "I suppose I had better be making my rounds of the city. By this time there must be a lost dog or a cat up a tree or something."

"Or Mrs. Yarp might have finished baking some apple strudel," laughed the Guardian. "I'm getting hungry too, and what I would like is a nice warm slice of pumpkin pie."

"OK, I will bring you one from the bakery when I'm done."

# Toto and the Cats of Oz

Patting his round mid-section, Faramant said, "No, no. You just hurry with your rounds and get on home to your dinner and get back here, so you can relieve me, so I can get on down town for my dinner! I may want pumpkin pie, but I do not *need* pumpkin pie!" Again he patted his round stomach, saying, "Now, go!"

"Don't push! Don't push," laughed the tall soldier as he put on his hat, picked up his gun, and went out the door.

After he left, the Guardian sat there awhile, thinking of the pumpkin pie he would be missing. Then he decided to take a look outside, across the beautiful green fields, to absorb their restful spirit. He sauntered over to the gate, took one look, and stepped back behind the wall again.

"Pumpkins?!" he exclaimed, leaning against the wall for support.

Then he decided to peek again. Surely his stomach was deceiving his eyes. There had never been pumpkins outside the gate before. Besides, they grew in the Winkie Country, not around the Emerald City.

But there they were. They certainly looked real. He stood for fully a minute, staring at them. Then he opened the gate, and with tentative steps, approached the closest of them. He leaned over it and it suddenly exploded, a cat springing from it, straight at him, snarling, with bared claws and teeth. At the same time all the other pumpkins erupted into spitting, mewling cats, most of whom streaked for the open gate.

"Stop! You can't do that!" shouted Faramant, trying

# The Fall of the Emerald City

to evade the furious cats that had him hemmed in.

"What makes you think they can't?" demanded a big blue cat. "You're not going to stop any cat. I am arresting you by order of the Royal Cat, Joom."

Bravely, the Guardian countered, "What is the meaning of this?"

"You'll find out soon enough," growled another cat, while Big Blue growled, "Come along."

Surrounded by fierce looking teeth and claws, Faramant had no choice but to do so.

Going through the gates, the cats pulled them tight shut behind themselves, locked them, and left one of their number as the new Guardian of the Gates.

Our old friend, and the true Guardian, shuddered at the thought.

However, once inside, the sight that greeted his eyes was even worse. Every citizen of the Emerald City that was on the streets was being accosted by a cat jumping upon his shoulders. Once there, he would dig in his claws a little and threaten worse if that Ozite would not obey him.

Looking up the street, Faramant could see that many of the cats had already reached the Palace. Fortunately, it looked like someone had succeeded in closing and locking the doors before the cats had reached them. So now a crowd of felines sat around the front doors yowling.

Behind those doors, word had been carried to the Wizard of the unexplainable attack by the cats. At the time, he happened to be talking to Tik-Tok and the

# Toto and the Cats of Oz

Shaggy Man. Thinking quickly, the Wizard began to wind the mechanical man's mechanism so he would not run down during this emergency. While doing so, he gave him hurried instructions, "Go to the balcony over the front entrance. Start talking to those cats. Try to find out what they are up to. Keep them busy, and keep them from making any trouble if you can."

As the round copper man hurried out, the Wizard continued speaking rapidly, now to the Shaggy Man. Then each went this own way, the Shaggy Man, to fulfill the Wizard's instructions, the Wizard to pick up from his workroom things that he thought might be needed. From there, he went to the front of the Palace to join his mechanical friend.

Tik-Tok did not seem to be having much luck in quieting the cats. They were only a small number out of the total that had invaded the Emerald City, but they were enough to make a crowd. They kept chanting, "We want Ozma," in a way that was not a very pleasant sounding refrain. Every time Tik-Tok tried to say something, they just shouted all the louder.

When the Wizard appeared on the balcony, they quieted some, but still a person would have had to yell to be heard above their cat calls. However, the Wizard had equipped himself with one of his voice magnifiers and when he spoke, it was as rolling thunder. "Ozma is away from the Emerald City, and I am the Great Oz, ruling in her place and in her name. Now, what is this all about?"

For awhile, as his voice echoed and reechoed, the cats were silent. Finally, a couple of ringleaders began

# The Fall of the Emerald City

calling again, "Bring us Ozma!" Other voices cried out for equal treatment. A general babble of sound developed until one silky, soft, buff-colored cat stepped out in front of the others. Although he was smaller than most, he was treated with special regard and his neighbors began to call out, "Let Honey Cat speak!" Soon, the voices of all the other cats faded away.

In the silence, that one, beautiful, silky-voiced cat spoke. It was immediately obvious that it was not only the color of his coat that gave him his name. The tone of his speech was truly that of fine honey, a sweetness that attracted.

"Behold this throng of gathered cats. Not one, but what he or she has sat softly upon some Ozian lap, purring contentedly. Why then are they come in violent protest, taking over the city, subduing the Guard and the Army? Such gentle creatures would not initiate such action unless their list of complaints was quite grievous, indeed. Hear then what they have to say!"

With that the cats broke out into thunderous cheers, calling out, "Hear, hear!"

As silence returned, the tawny cat continued: "I would not burden you with all their individual complaints. Such a list would extend completely around the walls of this fair city, itself. From where we stand, one could begin writing, and the writing would go on and on, stretching up and down every street of this iniquitous metropolis, winding its way, finally, to the walls, and on around them and back to this very spot. Yet the list would not be finished. It grows and grows. There is no end to the

# Toto and the Cats of Oz

list of charges. *But*, it can all be condensed down to the fact that you humans run everything. You are in charge. All the laws are made to suit you. No one ever considers us cats."

"Oh, but we do!" exclaimed the Wizard. "We have cats in the palace who live here as equals. Even some of Ozma's chief advisors are feline. Look at the Cowardly Lion and the Hungry Tiger."

"Yeah," responded several voices, "token cats."

"House cats!" jeered others.

"You call those cats?"

"They could gobble us in a single bite, and probably would if they had the chance."

"You see? That is the point," continued the buff-colored cat. "Look now at your one or two exceptions! Do you call them a great advance for catdom? Of what benefit are they for any other cat? Those two are not even cats. You use them as symbols to which you can point with heavy pride while all the real cats in the Kingdom are held in subjugation. They simply help you to rule Oz for the benefit of humans *and* to the detriment of real cats.

"You do not make laws to protect the rights of cats. People do not trust us as equals. Until laws are made to protect us, we are nothing but second class citizens. We have the responsibilities but none of the privileges of citizenship in Oz. People cannot know what it is like for us because all of you see it only from your own favored position."

As he stopped for a breath, the Wizard interrupted:

# The Fall of the Emerald City

"But, in an ideal fairyland like ours, there are no great needs. All you want is yours for the asking. No one needs any special laws to protect him."

"Oh, how you wound me," cried the silky cat. "In words you justify the deeds that never can be made right! Think you, sir, that any laws passed by humans can ever be fully fair for the feline world? What we need is representation. This is one of the oldest rules of democracy—no laws without representation."

"But Ozma could not possibly expand her Council to include every kind of creature in the Land of Oz— cats, dogs, mice, flying monkeys, Hammerheads, Fiddlecumjigs, spiders . . . " The Wizard took a quick breath. "To count them all would make a list as long as yours—clear around the city."

"We cannot speak for the rest of them," declared Honey Cat. "All we can say is that *we* are not fairly represented. For that reason alone, the laws are discriminatory. They are discriminatory against us!"

"Oh, stop the talk!" meowed a new voice from the hallway behind the Wizard. "You could go on like that till doomsday and never accomplish anything. These humans don't care! The time for talk is over. Now is the time for action!"

Turning to see who had spoken, the Wizard was faced by a ragged looking black cat that he recognized immediately as Joom. In body, a little larger than average, his head was of even a larger proportion. He showed signs of many fights. Both ears were notched, there were places where the hair would barely grow, and there were

# Toto and the Cats of Oz

*He was, indeed, strange and sinister looking.*

scars upon his head. From his too flat face, bright eyes shone with a strange light, accenting their exaggerated size. Two straps were about his body. Tucked under them was an iron rod, even longer than the cat. He was, indeed, strange and sinister looking.

"Hah, hah," he laughed. "You did not think you could lock this place tight enough to keep cats out, did you?"

While Joom spoke, the Wizard calmly reached into his black bag and pulled out a large hand mirror. The back and frame of it were engraved with many mysterious symbols, and as he held it, he tilted it so as to receive the light of the sun and reflect it back upon Joom and those cats that were with him. After mumbling a few magical

# The Fall of the Emerald City

syllables, the Wizard said, "This mirror is good for many things, Joom, but right now it is reversing the rays of the sun and they are freezing you quite still."

No sooner spoken than the scruffy black cat stopped all motion and stood stiff and still. Then the Wizard turned the rays of the mirror upon the crowd of snarling and unruly cats below the balcony, but they seemed quite unaffected by it, except for Honey Cat who jumped all around, successfully trying to avoid its bright beam.

Then the harsh laugh of Joom was heard again, "Hah, Ha! You said it would freeze me, so I obliged and stood still for a few moments, just for the fun of it." Then, advancing toward the Wizard, he continued more severely, "Now you had better yield to me without any more nonsense!"

But the Wizard was not beaten yet. One hand was already in his black bag, and as Joom came close to him, he pulled out a bottle, uncapped it and quickly sprinkled a bit of it upon the cat.

All that happened was that the dark feline shook himself. In doing so, some of the powder, then, fell upon flowers in a green pot next to him, and in the flash of an eye, those flowers and the pot were reduced to nearly microscopic size.

Shrinking powder, huh?" sneered Joom disdainfully. "Didn't you understand me?" And now he yelled, "Take these two to the cellar, and if they give you any trouble, rough up the little Wizard a bit."

Just then the Shaggy Man burst breathlessly onto the balcony. In his hand he held a horseshoe.

# Toto and the Cats of Oz

"Well, if it isn't Joom," he said in a most friendly manner. "Haven't seen you for several days. And some more lovely cats. Now this is well met. Let's ..."

At that point Joom broke in, snarling in a way that sent chills up the back of both Shaggy and the Wizard, "Cut the routine! No magic will work against us—not even your stupid love magnet. Yes, yes! I know what that is. Well, it won't work." Then, noting the perplexed look on the Shaggy Man's face, Joom broke into laughter again.

"Hah, hah! You all think you are so perfect and so safe. Oh, ho, ho! Did we ever pull a good one on you! You think you can solve everything with a little magic here and there. I'm here to tell you, 'This is one time you cannot.' We cats are all under a spell that no magic can work upon! Oh, hah, hah, ha! And now we have you right where we want you. There are only two things that would make my victory more complete—your little, ah, Queen and Dorothy." Then, with sudden vicious anger Joom lashed out at the Wizard, "Where are they?"

"I would not tell you even if I did know," answered the stout little Wizard.

"Oh, I'm sure you know," sneered Joom, "and, as for telling me? We shall see!"

At a motion from Joom, one of the big guard cats jumped upon the Wizard's back and began digging in his claws.

"You will speak soon enough," said Joom with a grim little laugh. "I already have taken Toto as a hostage to guarantee the proper responses from those two little girls. So, whether you speak or not, it is only a matter of time."

Bravely, the Wizard said not a word. In his silence, the cat might have hurt him badly, but in his wisdom about magic, it soon occurred to him that if magic could not be used to hurt these cats, then it should not be able to help them either. That thought ignited a plan in his mind. So he began to show his pain, struggling a bit and crying out. Finally, as though in desperation, he exclaimed, "Enough! Enough! All right, make that cat stop. I can tell you what you wish."

"That's more like it," snarled Joom, and then, more slowly, "All right. You may stop with the claws now. And Mr. Wizard, what can you tell me?"

Breathing heavily, the Wizard said, "Ozma and Dorothy are on trips—separately."

"Now that is a good beginning," spoke Joom with a sarcastic sound to his voice, "but I need more than that!"

"Well, actually, I do not know much more than that."

"Surely," snapped the scruffy cat, glancing at the cat that had previously attacked the Wizard, "they told you where they were going."

Quickly, and before the other cat had taken more than a couple of steps, the Wizard answered, "Not exactly, but there are instruments in my laboratory that could help us find them."

The prospect of entering the Wizard's laboratory made a gleam come into Joom's eyes as he gloated, "Now that's more like it. Come guards," and in silky tones, "We will take them wherever they please. It is your turn, Mr.

# Toto and the Cats of Oz

Wizard. Lead away."

Surrounded by a dozen cats, the Wizard set out toward his own laboratory, whispering to Tik-Tok and the Shaggy Man, "If you stick very close to me, we can give them a bit of a surprise when we reach there."

Following the twists and turns of the palace halls and staircase, they finally reached their destination. There they all paused at the door while the Wizard mumbled a few mystic phrases and the door opened.

"Come in," he said, beckoning to the cats and turning toward shelves of powders and chemicals on the left.

As he did so, Joom snarled, "Stay away from those. They won't do you any good anyway. Get started on finding those two girls."

So, reluctantly turning the other direction and stepping between Shaggy and Tik-Tok, he said, "Let me see. We will need to move this bench over here." As he spoke, he and his friends were right in front of his special Magic Hoops and he placed the bench between them and the cats. This was just enough to keep the cats from stopping them as the trio hopped through the Hoops, with the Wizard saying, "Take us to Glinda's."

As they did so, the three friends could see cats hurtling toward them, but the Wizard's plan worked just as expected. Since magic could have no effect upon these cats, the magic of the hoops could not be used to help them follow the Wizard and his friends. The cats copied his words: "Take us to Glinda's," but, of course, they were balked and only remained standing in the now empty Hoops, hissing and spitting in anger.

# Chapter 14

# Alexander's Explanation

he path that Toto and the big gray cat, Alexander, had found took them deep into the green woods. At first, it had been a light and airy forest, but the further they went, the darker and darker it became. Then the path began to climb. All day they followed it, winding through the somber, dark woods, always climbing higher into the mountains. Now, toward evening, the trees thinned and they found themselves on the edge of an upland meadow.

"Let's stop here for the night. It is a beautiful spot," puffed Toto, a little out of breath, as he flopped down on the matting of needles.

"Ah, why not go on? It's lighter now that we're out o' the woods. Once we're over that hump up there we might be able t' start down the other side—before dark even."

"Well, let's rest a little anyway," panted Toto. "I'll get my breath in a minute."

"Oh ho," laughed Alexander. "I get it. You're wearin' out faster'n I am. I f'rget about you flatlanders not bein' able to do these hills so good. Bein' raised in the mountains, I'm use t' all this climbin'."

"Mountains? I thought you said you were from the waterfront."

"Yeah. It's really both. I was born in the mountains. My mother was a tough alley cat that had made her way to a lumber camp and my dad was a wildcat. As I grew up, I learned how t' catch rides on the trucks t' the harbor where there were always lots o' fish. Got t' spending about half my time in the mountains, an' half on the docks."

"Hmm," breathed Toto as his eyes closed and he drifted off in sleep, a sleep that lasted all through the night. Even the fresh mountain air did not awaken him until late the next morning. Alexander was already up, sitting at the edge of the forest, looking across the meadow at the snow-covered mountain peaks towering above it.

Toto stretched himself a few times and trotted over beside his new friend. Hearing him, but not turning his head, Alexander drew a deep breath and said, "Ain't it beautiful? Once ya've lived in mountains ya c'n never be satisfied without 'em."

"They really are impressive and very lovely," replied Toto, "But something bothers me. Even though I cannot be sure what I remember and what I do not, I feel like saying, 'I have never seen snow in Oz before.'"

"It may be unusual here, but mountains like these ju's ought'a have snow on 'em."

Changing the conversation to a more urgent concern, Toto asked "What's for breakfast?"

Jumping up and turning to stand right in front of Toto, Alexander exclaimed, "Ya won't believe it. The craziest

# Alexander's Explanation

thing I ever saw! But come. Take a look for yourself."
And the big cat headed off, down the meadow a way to
lead Toto into a stand of trees on the hillside.

"There! Did ya ever see anything like that afore?"
he asked, pointing to a tree in the center of the grove.
It was hung all over with pails, pails that were not just
placed there, but that were growing from the branches.
They were of various sizes and colors. The smaller ones
tended to be greenish; larger ones, yellowish; and the
largest ones were mostly red, orange or brown.

Toto began to chuckle as Alexander excitedly
continued, "I couldn't open the littler ones, but I opened
a couple o' the red ones, and ya'd never guess what I
found inside!"

"Oh yes I would," laughed Toto. "There were
sandwiches, chicken or potato salad, fruit punch and hot
soup, all growing attached to the sides of those baskets."

"How'd ya know? Have ya already been up and
around?"

"No, but these grow all around the Land of Oz.
Lunch Bucket Trees are very convenient for travelers,
you know."

"Well, I'll be! Is the stuff safe to eat?"

"Of course it is," replied the dog as he trotted over to
where the baskets sat that Alexander had already picked.
Inside, it was just as Toto had said. At one end grew a
container full of a hot soup with a beef-like flavor. At the
other end, another container had in it an ice cold liquid
that tasted like limeade. In between were two tomato
sandwiches, a container of leafy salad with oil oozing

out of it just like a dressing, and one chicken drumstick — at least it looked like a drumstick and it tasted like one. Everything grew, attached by stems, to the inside of the basket.

As they started eating the cat kept muttering to himself, "I can't believe it. I can't believe it!"

When they finished, Toto showed him how the ends of some of the branches would make excellent spoons for humans to use with their soup, while the large leaves could serve them as napkins.

By now, Alexander was mumbling, "Amazing, amazing!"

After eating for awhile, Alexander spoke up again, "Now look there! Ya've gone and done it again."

"Done what?"

"Ya don't really remember who ya are, where ya live, what ya're doin' or nothin', but I show ya a strange tree, an' ya start right out tellin' me all about it jus' like ya remember everything."

"Why yes," Toto responded, "that is strange. It just seemed as natural as anything to know all about Lunch-Bucket Trees, but I still do not really remember anything that happened to me before I met those mice on the road yesterday."

Having eaten everything out of the pails, Toto showed Alexander how to dispose of the pails by eating them. They were rather leathery, but, in a way, they reminded the cat of the fruit chews dock hands had occasionally shared with him back home. For fear they might not find other food for the rest of the day, they picked two more

# Alexander's Explanation

buckets, one that each could carry hanging around his neck. Then they started off across the meadow and over the hillside into the rough and rocky mountains.

As they trotted along, both of them were quiet for a while. Finally Toto broke the silence: "I can't figure this out. When we met on the road yesterday, you seemed to know me. But there is nothing about you that seems familiar to me."

"Well, y'r a little befuddled, aren't ya? Ya don't seem t' remember anythin' too well."

"Yes, but you say you are a stranger to Oz, while I live in its Capital, this Emerald City, so how did we know each other at all?"

"Ah-h, we gotta face it some time. The fact is, I was your guard."

"Really?" and Toto sounded quite surprised. "The mice told me I lived in the palace, but I didn't know I was important enough to rate a guard all my own!"

"No, stupid. Not that kind of guard. I wasn't protectin' ya. I was keepin' ya from escapin'!"

"So that's what you want!" cried Toto with a sudden pang of fear. He turned, then, to run across a rocky slope.

Before he had taken more than a few steps, the big cat called out, "No, no, no! I've quit. I'm on y'r side now. This whole business is nothin' but a mess!"

Pausing and turning to look at the cat, Toto said, "Well, you seem like a good sort, and I would really like to hear you out. So, do not come any closer, but start telling me what this is all about."

"OK." And true to his word, Alexander moved no

closer, but hopping up on a small boulder, began his story with a question. "Unhh, d'ya remember that other cat named Joom? He was black an' scruffy an' sorta 'n odd ball."

"Joom?" Yes," answered Toto, sitting down on a scraggly little patch of grass amongst the rocks. "He seems to be a fuzzy kind of memory to me—but all I can recall is what you just said—black and odd."

"Well, he set out t' conquer Oz. He called it a revolution o' down-trodden cats. I thought it was a great thing at first. Ya have no idea how mis'rable a cat's life c'n be— worse 'n a dog's life! I thought I would be strikin' a blow f'r freedom. It even sounded like it'd be fun. In America we could never do it, but in Oz? He made it sound as easy as pie.

"Some chance! I've had enough! Why, he was down right brutal. An' he wasn't int'rested in freedom f'r cats at all. He just wanted power. I heard him laugh his cackling laugh and say he'd teach them all a thing or two. An' the way he said it was utterly cruel.

"Why, he ain't even a cat, really. He's some sort o' magician that c'n transform himself into a cat. When he's a person, he's an ugly ol' guy, stooped and with a distorted lookin' face—enough to scare the bejabbers out'a ya!"

"Hm'm, yes," interrupted Toto. "Vaguely, I seem to remember something like that. It makes me feel kind of uneasy. But I do not remember what it is all about."

"Yeah," responded the cat, "it should make you feel uneasy. That Joom is dangerous! Ya shoulda' seen what

# Alexander's Explanation

he got the cats t' do in th' Emerald City! I was ashamed. They were downright brutal—stickin' their claws in people jus' t' hear 'em scream! They were nothin' but a wild mob. I'd gone inta it 'cause I thought cats in Oz were really gettin' a bad deal, but, if we're goin' t' behave worse'n people, then we might as well leave everything in their hands.

"Anyway, it was so bad, I jus' decided I'd give up an' leave the first time I'd have a chance. Findin' you was an unexpected bonus. We'll have t' hide, an' these mountains might be jus' the place."

"We certainly seem isolated and out-of-the-way up here, all right," responded the dog. "But tell me more. How did a cat like you from America happen to get mixed up with a magical cat from Oz?"

"I use t' know him when he was jus' 'n ordinary cat in America named Binkie. But, like I say, Joom ain't really a cat. He's some ugly old magician from Oz an' I don' actually understand it at all! An' I keep wonderin' what's happened t' Binkie. It's all so confusin'."

The big cat shook himself a bit, took a long leonine stretch, cleared his throat, and said, "Let me start over. Me 'n Binkie 'n Honey Cat was friends on the piers in Seattle. They an' some o' the others lived in the warehouses aroun' the waterfront there, but I jus' lived with 'em part time. My real home was up in the mountains. Like I say, my dad was a wildcat I never knew, 'n my mom was the pet o' the loggin' camp. There was only me 'n my sister born that winter, 'n she didn't last it through.

"I'd ride aroun' on the delivery truck that brought

147

supplies t' camp. One time I rode clear back t' town an' on down t' the warehouse near the waterfront where the supplies came from. There I discovered fish! M-m-m-m! An' that's where I met Binkie an' Honey Cat an' the others.

"Then one day 'bout a month ago, we heard that a fishin' boat Binkie had gone onta had broken up at sea. Some of the crew were saved, but no sign of a cat, an' we thought sure that Binkie was a goner. Then, lo 'n behold, a few days later he turns up again, but now he said we should call him 'Joom.' An' he wasn't the same ol' Binkie at all.

"Ya see, here was a cat with the body of Binkie, but he had some'un else's personality. An' I've been wonderin' ever since, 'Where's the real Binkie?' It bothers me, an' that's part o' why I can't go along with this Joom any more.

"But I'm gettin' ahead o' the story. Joom started tellin' us all 'bout this wonderful Land o' Oz 'n the big cat revolution that was underway, an' he convinced us we oughta be a part of it.

"I think someplace in that Binkie head o' his he was rememberin' how he could lick jus' about anythin' but me, an' what a tough crew the rest o' the waterfront cats was. An' he was thinkin' 'bout Honey Cat bein' able t' talk the skin right off a rat. Oh, Honey Cat's got a gift there, he does, but 'spite o' all that's happened, he still believes in Joom for the sake o' Binkie. An' he'll do just about whatever that mean cat wants him to.

"Honey Cat's one o' the best — good-natured, heart o' gold. He'd do anythin' f'r ya. He al'ys wants t' help everyone. An' once he knows ya, it's hard f'r him t' believe bad about ya."

"Umm," grunted Toto. "I can just kind of remember bits of this, but it's all pretty hazy. I wish I knew what has happened to me."

"Hey now, that's an easy one," replied the cat. "You're under both a spell 'n a counter-spell. When Joom took ya captive, he put ya under a spell o' forgetfulness, an' then he took ya t' the Spellin' Bee who put ya under a Counter-spell that makes it impossible f'r any further magic t' have any effect on ya."

"But I remember the last couple of days just fine, and yet everything before that is practically a blank."

"Maybe that's because o' the bump ya got when ya fell out o' the Holder's wagon. I don't know much about how this magic stuff works, but it seems reasonable."

"No," replied the dog, "that's not very likely."

"How do ya know what's likely and what's not?" asked the cat.

"Hm, hm," chuckled Toto. "Good question. For some reason it just does not seem right to me. Little things like that slip right out without me even knowing where they come from. The more we talk about it, the more familiar it seems to me. But it's also making me dizzy. Let's get going."

As he said these last words, Toto jumped up and started out. Alexander hopped off the rock on which he had been sitting and fell into step beside the little dog. Thus the two comrades continued on towards Glinda's, little realizing what a surprise faced them at the end of this day.

# Chapter 15

# Christmas Valley

t was late afternoon by the time Ozma, Uncle Henry, Scraps and the Sawhorse crossed the last rise in the pass entering Christmas Valley. Ozma had the Sawhorse stop so all could enjoy the sweeping view of that magical and wondrous vale, nestled among the snow clad mountains. No sooner had they stopped than a strange, dark, bent creature stood in their way, blocking their advance.

For a moment no one said anything, but then Uncle Henry hopped off the back of the Sawhorse, strode toward the figure, and wrapping his arms around the little man's shoulders, said, "I kinda expected that, with Ozma among us, Santa'd send his chief deputy out t' meet us, ya ol' scalawag!"

With a resounding pat on Henry's back, the one he addressed answered, "It's good to see you again." Then separating, he bowed to Ozma, saying, "Welcome. I bring you warmest greetings from Neclaus. He awaits you in his workshop."

"Thank you, Peter," responded Ozma, recognizing the immortal's name for Santa Claus. "Hop up here on the Sawhorse and away we'll go."

As Peter paused, the wooden steed said, "Go right ahead. Everyone else is up there."

"Oh, if you don't want us riding you, we could all walk," countered the princess with a little smile.

"Naw. That's okay. I was just being boorish."

Black Peter was a Knook, a member of the race of immortals assigned the job of caring for all the animals of the world. He had long been Santa's chief assistant and, as usual, was dressed in the fine garb of olden days. He wore short puffy pants and a tight sleeveless jacket, both made of bright green and red striped velvet. His shirt was of white silk with embroidered sleeves and a stiffened ruff at the neck. Tight green leggings lead down to soft red leather shoes. A short cape of red and green satin was loosely thrown over his shoulders. Across the front of his jacket hung a gold chain, and a slender birch rod was in his hand. All was topped by a jaunty, jeweled green beret with an ostrich feather stuck in it.

While Peter was getting settled into place, the others had a chance to look at the view. It was a breathtaking vista, sweeping across fields of snow to the graceful chalets that made up Santa's little village. Beyond stood the white-tipped peaks that virtually surrounded this high valley.

Naturally, they were awed by the beauty of this scene even though it was not new to them. They had all been here a few years earlier when Santa Claus had the grand opening of his new Oz workshop. This was not a replacement for the two he already had, one at

Earth's North Pole and another at the Laughing Valley of Hohaho far to the south of Oz. Rather, over the years his work load had grown and grown. Necessity required that he add more floor space to his workshops. Beyond that, because of the distant vastness of the range of his duties, he also needed a pick-up point located far from his other two installations. Upon running out of gifts when he was in Oz, he would no longer have to go all the way back to one of the other factories to reload.

This location, in the highest mountains of Oz and on the border between the red Quadling Country and the green environs of the Emerald City made an ideal location for his new regional headquarters. Although snow was rare in Oz, he had covered Christmas Valley and its peaks with magical white crystals that were never cold and never melted and yet could easily be compacted for snowballs and the building of snow forts.

The speedy Sawhorse brought them to Santa's Workshop in a matter of moments. As their steed skidded to a stop in the snow, Peter dismounted to lead them into a vast space full of toys, work benches, miscellaneous parts, tools and busy people. There were ryls, elves, knooks, fairies, pixies and wood nymphs busily at work, each on his or her own project. As the visitors looked around, they could see a familiar figure coming toward them. He was dressed in red with woolly white trim and a bushy white beard.

"Ah ho, fair Queen Ozma and Henry and Scraps and the Sawhorse. How good to see you again!" he called out cheerily.

# Christmas Valley

"Neclaus," responded the little Queen as she ran to be enfolded in his great arms, "I'd hoped to find you here."

"Easily done," replied the old gentleman. "I was at the North Pole, but when Peter alerted me that Ozma and her friends were on their way here, the fleetness of my reindeer brought me here even before you could make it. Come, let us go on over to the lodge."

Traipsing through the snow, Scraps could not resist grabbing a handful and squeezing it into a ball which she immediately threw at the Sawhorse. With a snort, he responded by kicking wild flurries of it into her face, not to mention into the faces of everybody else in the group. Soon, the whole party was throwing fluffy white balls at each other. Then, with a great deal of laughing, it was over as suddenly as it had begun and the little group had entered the main building.

It was just like walking into a Swiss chalet at Christmas time. The rooms were big and high with open woodwork everywhere. Across the ample entrance-way was a huge curving staircase giving access to the surrounding balcony. Besides the one large Christmas tree cradled in the sweep of the stairway, smaller ones were in each corner of the entry room.

Ozma started: "Neclaus, old friend, I wish we could properly enjoy these delightful surroundings. However, we are here on urgent business. Oz is …"

But Santa interrupted her with a finger to the side of his nose as he said, "Hush now. I know about the trouble that Joom is causing, but let us await some others who are yet to arrive. If I am not mistaken some of them will have important news for us. In the meantime, relax, enjoy the evening."

"Well now, that's a bit hard t' do," exclaimed Uncle Henry, "when we're worryin' about what's happenin' t' the whole Kingdom."

"Of course it is," answered the jolly old man. "But for now, there isn't much else we can do."

Just then a busy little elf in green overalls bustled into the grand entryway. Santa turned to him and said, "Ah good Jule, you have the room assignments for our guests, I'm sure."

"Indeed, I do, Kris. Princess Ozma, of course, will have room 200, that fine room right over the front entrance. Uncle Henry will be in Room 212, down the hall and around the corner. It too, is one of our best. And, of course, the sleepless Scraps and Sawhorse are free to roam where they will or stop where they will."

"Ah shaw! I don't need no special room," objected Henry.

"Ho, ho," laughed Santa, "You may not need it, but it's yours for tonight. Ho, ho. No arguing."

"All right."

"But, for awhile," said Santa, "we will all go ahead into the Fireplace Room, after I introduce you to our chief of staff, here."

However, before he could say more a dark shadow fell across Scraps, who reacted by falling backward. Everyone screamed, and there lay the Patchwork Girl on the floor, one leg in her face, the other bent under her, and one arm flailing in the air over her head and the other twisted under her and around to where its hand was laying on top of her on the other side.

Everyone tensed up until a shrill voice said, "I'm sorry, there was just such a delicious looking group of bugs by that light, I had to sweep them up. Didn't think about the shadow I'd create and its effect on you. Please, forgive me."

Then everyone could see a Great Southern Red Bat hanging from one of the beams above them.

Now, everyone laughed, Scraps the hardest of all. Santa said, "That's all right sir or madam, I think we've all recovered."

The bat replied, "Sir, it is, and I'm still sorry, but I'll leave you now," and he swooped down from the high beam and out the open window near the light that had attracted him in the first place.

The little elf ran over and closed the window with a bang and a click.

With everything calmed down, Santa, sweeping his arm toward the active little fellow, said, "This is Jule Nissen who makes all arrangements for the cleaning and staffing of all these buildings, and who also does all that is necessary for any visitors we have." Then he introduced the visitors, one by one.

When he was done, Scraps, ever bold and unconstrained, said to Santa, but he called you, 'Kris.' What did he mean by that?"

"Oh, ho, ho. I have many names. Each peoples have their own special one for me. Originally I was known as 'Saint Nicholas.' In America, that was elided into

'Santa Claus' and in the Netherlands and Belgium, into Sinterklaas. In France they have called me, 'Pere Noel.' In Scotland, I was known as 'MacNicolaus.' In England I'm often called 'Father Christmas.' Among many Slavs, it is some form of Mikolaja. The name 'Kris Kringle' originated among the Pennsylvania Dutch in the 1820s, where I was also known as 'Belsnickle.' Earlier, in their homeland of Germany, I was called 'Pelz-nickle,' and in parts of Hungary, Pleznickel, meaning 'fur-skin Nicholas.' And there are many other names for me."

"Amazing," said Scraps. Who would have guessed you had so many names?"

With that settled, Santa led the way through a great arch into a large room with a huge fireplace dominating one side of it and said, "Here you can make yourselves comfortable until bedtime." Then he turned toward a door that was just opening and said, "Ho, ho, now. What is this?" And a lovely little person in light green robes billowing around her darted toward Santa and quickly whispered something in his ear. In response, he stood up and, in a slightly mysterious voice, said, "Ha, ho. There now, you all settle down and warm yourselves here. We should be back before bedtime. Ho, ho, and now we're on our way. I must go to greet a couple more of our friends right now," and his deep chuckle rolled back to them as he went off down the hallway with Jule Nissen right behind him.

# Chapter 16

# Two More Arrivals

y noon, Toto and Alexander had crossed the wide expanse of rocks only to find there was no path continuing deeper into the green-hued mountains.

Now they had to pick their way through a heavy growth of bushes, a task baffling to the little dog, but welcomed by the larger cat. With experience bred in the mountains of the Puget Sound country, he was quickly able to find the right places to squeeze through. But, even with the way shown to him, the dog struggled. Alexander slipped between branches, but when Toto tried to follow, he would find he had not hit exactly the same spot, pushing instead into a fresh tangle. Then he would try to back up, like as not get into a dead end, and spend fifteen minutes getting untangled.

At first, stops for rest were frequent. Gradually however, Alexander learned which brushes were giving Toto the worst trouble and would make sure he stayed put until the little dog was coming through the right gap, and the stops became less frequent.

Late in the afternoon, starting out from a brief rest, Alexander cried, "Hey! Look there. Through that gap ahead, there's a red mountain! What 'a ya make 'a that?"

And sure enough, although snow covered, the rocks showing through were certainly red.

"It is to be expected," was Toto's reply.

"What d'ya mean? A red mountain in the midst o' green ones. Why?"

"I'm not just certain, but that is what I would expect, and I'll bet there are more red ones around it!"

"There ya go again. Ya know it, but ya don't. Somehow, we're gonna have t' get ya straightened out."

They continued on toward the gap where the red mountain showed. Dusk was drawing down upon them by the time they reached it and found themselves looking out upon a great snow-covered valley with a little village, lights a-gleam, right in the center. Around it towered snow-topped mountains cut by rocky ribs. The rocks of the nearest of the mountains were green, but on the far side they were red.

"Yup," declared Alexander. "Ya were right — it is surrounded by more red mountains."

"There must be a reason," said the dog. "But I sure don't know what it is now."

Looking down into the valley, they saw a big red sleigh drawn by four little horses approaching them at a great speed. In a twinkling, sleigh, steeds and driver were in front of them, and the two friends saw that it was not horses, but reindeer that drew the sleigh, and the driver was all dressed in red with white fur trim and a bushy white beard.

"I-it can't be!" exclaimed Alexander. "Everybody

# Two More Arrivals

knows he's just a fairy tale!"

"And this is a fairy country," interjected Toto, "so here he is. That is … ah-h. Goodness! I know who he is, but I just cannot remember his name or anything about him."

By this time the man in red had descended from the sleigh, and with a jolly, deep laugh, he said,

"Ho-ho-ho.
Bless my soul.
I believe
I found Toto!"

"Were you looking for me ?" the dog replied.

"Everyone has been looking for you," replied the merry old man.

Turning quickly to Alexander, Toto anxiously asked, "Is that good or bad?"

"I think it's good," was his answer. "I can't think of anyone who wouldn't like to have Santa Claus lookin' for him," and then whispering to Toto, "if that really is who he is."

"Indeed! That is exactly who I am," laughed the old gentleman. "Toto and I are old friends." Then turning to the little dog, he continued, "Surely you did not have to ask Alexander if it was safe to have me looking for you?"

"I do not really know," he answered. "I seem to have forgotten everything. Yet, bits of it keep coming back. I know I've seen you before, and I think I like you, but that is all I can say for certain. In fact, until Alexander called you, 'Santa Claus,' I couldn't even remember your name."

"Ha! That's rich!" exclaimed Alexander. "Everywhere in the world they know the name of this man!" Then, hesitantly, and with some of his boldness disappearing, he asked the bearded man, "It is you, isn't it?"

"That depends on who you think I am. The fairies call me Neclaus, but mortals usually call me Chris Kringle or Father Christmas, or a multitude of other names. In your own land, Alexander, you call me Santa Claus."

"I never thought I'd ever see ya f'r real," muttered the cat in an awed voice.

"Ha, ha. I am real enough," declared Santa Claus.

"An' ya know my name!"

"Of course I do," stated the old gentleman as he hopped back into the sleigh. "It is my business to know names and who is where and what they are doing. But ho now! 'Tis time for us to head for my office. Come along."

Toto and Alexander climbed up beside him, nestling into the warm folds of his fuzzy red and white blanket. As they did so, Santa gave a quick whistle and the reindeer started off down the white slope. This time they went at the slower pace of ordinary steeds. As Santa explained, their usual speed might be too breath-taking for mortal beings.

Alexander was brimming with curiosity, so as soon as they had settled and the sleigh was under way, he said, "Ya know Santa, I've got one question. How in the world can ya get t' every house on Earth in one night?"

# Two More Arrivals

"Ho ho," laughed the good elf, "I could never do it without my reindeer. Nothing mortals have yet developed can go as fast as they do. You saw how fast we approached you?"

"Yup, that was about as fast as I've ever seen anything move," replied the cat.

"Well, that was just slow speed," replied Santa. "On Christmas Eve, they and I too, move so fast, no eye can see us. But that's not all. I also have a kind of magic that makes it possible for me to play tricks with time, so that I get to the next country before I left the last one. couldn't ever do it otherwise."

"Wheeuw," whistled Alexander. "Now that's somethin'!" Then whispering to the dog, he asked, "D'ya celebrate Christmas here in Oz, too?"

"Why, of course. After all, Santa Claus is one of us."

"Ya mean he's from Oz? I thought he lived at the North Pole and this would just be a branch office."

"No, it's not because he lives here, but because he is one of our kind of people. He is an immortal like the people of Oz and the elves and ryls and fairies."

"Hey!" exclaimed Alexander. "How come y're remembering all this?"

"I am not sure why. I just do. In fact, when I stop to think about it," and now Toto began laughing as he spoke, "I am not even sure whether I remember it or not."

Santa Claus interjected, "As a matter of fact, Toto, you have it just right. Your memory works in some ways at least."

# Toto and the Cats of Oz

Gliding along through the snow, the runners of the sleigh made a pleasant shoosh-shoosh sound. The bells on the reindeers' harness rang a merry tune, and soon Santa Claus lead the others in a familiar old song:

"Dashing through the snow,
In a one horse open sleigh ..."

After they had sung three verses, Alexander surprised everyone, even himself, by singing out a verse he had made up on the spot:

"Skimming o'er the snow,
Fol'wing Santa's deer,
Ah, what a great grand show
To ride with Santa here,
Warmly tucked within
A swiftly flying sleigh
That brings us to a bright
    and shiny inn at end of day."

The others, including the reindeer, joined in the chorus of "Jingle Bells" again. By the time they were finished, sure enough, the deer had brought the sleigh to a stop right in front of the largest building in Christmas Valley, and it was bright and shiny with candles a-gleam in every one of its many windows.

Santa took them through the great, high front hall into the fireplace room where they found two humans, a giant stuffed doll, and a wooden sawhorse. These

# Two More Arrivals

immediately cried out, "Toto," and came rushing over to pick him up. For the time being, Alexander was ignored, Santa Claus forgotten.

"Thank goodness you are safe!"

"Where have you been?"

"What has happened?"

"So you are the visitor Santa had to go meet?"

These and other questions and exclamations flew thick and fast while both of the people and even Scraps took turns passing Toto from one to the other and petting him.

Finally, as they grew more quiet, Toto said, "You must be some of the humans with whom I live." There was a shocked silence that he momentarily filled with, "You all seem familiar to me, but I just do not remember everything."

Again, bedlam broke loose, with one saying this and another saying that:

"Oh! Poor Toto."

"What has Joom done to you?"

"Ozma will get your memory back for you."

"What's that cat, Alexander, doing here?"

"Is Joom around, too?"

When everyone ran out of breath, Toto began explaining that Alexander was a friend now, also fleeing from Joom, and that as far as they knew, that evil black cat was still in the Emerald City which he and the other cats had captured. He could not remember what Joom had done to him, nor much of anything. Partly he recognized them, but only dimly.

Their new questions were answered with uncertainties and more questions.

Soon Santa interrupted their discouraging attempts to help Toto remember. "Come now, enough of this. Tomorrow Ozma and I will see what we can do about Toto." Then, as some of his elves came through the door, he added in a confidential tone, "We elves have a little magic of our own, you know."

# Chapter 17

# By the Fireplace

ettling around the great fireplace, everyone was exclaiming about the warm and cozy feeling given by the presence of all the wreaths, tinsel, garlands and other decorations.

Toto, despite the mystery of his lost memory, was content. The others were simply pleased that he was safe. All cares were forgotten as talk turned to the joys of Christmas. After a few minutes of that Santa reminded them, "As important as this holiday is to me personally, you know, there are others who celebrate Kwanzaa or Hanukkah during this period of short days."

"'Course, there are," agreed Uncle Henry. "We kind o' forget 'bout those with different holidays from our own."

"Yes," added Ozma, "I have heard of those celebrations, but I hardly know anything about them."

Everyone looked around at everyone else.

"Crickity, I guess none of us know much about the customs of others," remarked Henry. "More's the pity."

At that moment the elves began bringing Christmas cheer for the guests — large pitchers of red or green

# Toto and the Cats of Oz

punch, gingerbread and sugar cookies cut like Christmas trees, wreaths, stars, angels, and fruit cake, candied orange peel, marzipan and many other goodies. Conversation returned to Christmas and then to Christmas Valley.

"How long is it, Santa? You've had this, here, workshop for about fifteen years now haven't you?" declared Uncle Henry.

"Almost exactly. It was August 1995. It had been getting hard to keep up with things at the other two."

"Three of them," said Alexander, "and I'd always thought there was just the one at the North Pole."

"Yes," laughed Santa, "on Earth, just that one. But here on Ozeria is where I started it all. My original workshop is in the Laughing Valley of Hohaho near the Great Forest of Burzee. I started by taking care of the children here. Only much later did I expand to Earth. Now my work has expanded so much that it takes three workshops to get it all done."

"What do ya mean, Ozeria?" asked Alexander.

Scraps laughed a comical little giggle and recited:

"Ozeria, is where we are.
Earth, is not home to Oz.
Magic is useless there.
Ozeria well hidden, 'cause
Only bewitching gets you here.
Or maybe something very belacoz."

"You silly stuffed mannequin," growled the Sawhorse. "Can't you ever resist those dumb rhymes?"

# By the Fireplace

In response, the Patchwork Girl stuck her tongue out and wiggled her fingers in her ears at him.

Alexander, trying to edge away from an argument, quickly interposed, "Yeah. I guess it was a bit of bewitchment when Joom brought me here. And I always thought magic was just in fairy tales."

"'Deedy," remarked Uncle Henry. "We are in a fairy land. Ozma is a fairy. There are others. Santa is an Immortal. And you probably haven't begun to see the strange beings that abound in Oz."

"I gotta admit, live wooden sawhorses and stuffed dolls! That's new to me."

Uncle Henry stretched just as Ozma stifled a yawn.

"It's been a long day," said Santa. "Perhaps it is time for Jule to show you to your rooms."

"Probably," mumbled the two of them.

Then Santa picked up a small ceramic Christmas tree and gave it a shake. It was a beautifully tuned bell. "Jule can hear that wherever he is and he should be here momentarily."

On the last word, a door on the far side of the room flew open and in dashed that very elf. He, quickly, bowed to Ozma and motioned to Uncle Henry and the two of them followed him out into the entryway and up the stairs. On the second floor they found that the elves had prepared a sweet and dainty room for Ozma, but a more rustic looking one for Uncle Henry, with a big old-fashioned four poster bed.

Toto and Alexander curled up, close to each other and not far from the great fireplace, while the Sawhorse and Scraps sat further away, safer for cotton and wood, whispering occasionally. Those two needed no sleep, but they stayed in the delightful Christmas atmosphere of the big room.

Elves and knooks and ryls came through from time to time on some errand or another. But one time the reindeer, Prancer, came in, shaking snow off his fur and rattling his antlers. He stood a ways from the fireplace, but was evidently enjoying its warmth. Although the snow itself was not cold, night at this high elevation brought a certain chill, and, in this climate, the reindeer had shed its winter coat.

"Good place for warming up," began the Patchwork Girl.

"Yup," grunted Prancer.

"Like this better than the North Pole?" queried the Sawhorse.

"Nope."

"Isn't it pretty cold up there?"

"Yup."

Scraps punched the Sawhorse in the side and whispered, "Guess he doesn't talk much."

"But he's got pretty good ears," said the reindeer. "Nope. I don't do a lot of talking, but I guess that's kind of rude some times. The North Pole. Now that is kind of isolated, but not nearly like it was when we first went up there. There are jets flying over all the time. You'd think they might disturb the Arctic silence, but they're so high up you hardly hear them. As a matter of fact, being the next fastest flying thing to us in all the world,

# By the Fireplace

it's something like having cousins flying by with their distant hum a kind of a friendly 'Hello.'"

"Interesting concept," remarked the Sawhorse.

"I've got another one," said Prancer. "Look at those logs, just kind of smoldering embers now."

"Umm-Hmm."

"It kind of reminds me of looking down into the stomach of a sleeping dragon."

"Ohh! Have you done that?" quavered the Patchwork Girl.

"N-no. But that's what I think it would look like."

"That's all well and good for you. But, for a lady of my composition, I'd prefer not even getting close enough to think about it."

"Me too!" exclaimed the Wooden Sawhorse as he backed further away from the fireplace.

"Didn't mean to alarm you," said the reindeer, shifting his feet a bit nervously. "Guess I didn't think about how threatening a fire could be to you two."

"S'okay," responded Scraps. "Each of us have our own little phobias. But tell us more about life at the North Pole."

They talked a few more minutes, then Prancer excused himself, "Better get back out. I'm on Night Patrol."

"What do you have to patrol around here?" asked the Sawhorse.

"Nothing really. I've never heard of anything going wrong, but just in case."

So the night went. An occasional conversation with

one of Santa's helpers passing through, long moments of silence, a few words passing between the two old friends, an occasional growl, whimper or mutter from the sleeping animals.

# Chapter 18

# Joom Discovered

he next morning everyone was up early. It had been late when they went to bed, but they were all so excited that no one could sleep very long. After all, here they were in Christmas Valley, one of Santa's workshops. And had he not promised to help Ozma cure Toto's memory problem today? And would they not go on to collect more magic workers to help overcome this dreadful Joom? It looked like a momentous day ahead for all.

When they gathered at the breakfast tables, Santa stood to give what was, for him, a very serious speech:

"As you well know, I do not usually interfere in the affairs of mortals. My business with the world is to bring Christmas cheer. It started with children. Now those children have grown up, and their children's children, and their children, and so on. But still I care for all of them, the grown up children as well as the little ones. I love them too much to try to dictate their lives. Yes, too much, even when I know what is best for them—*especially* when I know what is best. So I stay clear.

"But this time there is more at stake. I owe my very

171

existence to the help of the Immortals, particularly the wood nymphs, fairies, ryls and knooks. When the Immortal fairy, Ozma, needs my help, I cannot turn her away. The cause becomes even more urgent, however, when we consider how serious it would be if that evil Joom were to take over this beautiful fairyland." Laughing a bit, Santa continued, "Naturally, if he were to take over all of Oz, that would include Christmas Valley. Of course, I cannot let him do that, can I?"

"No, no. Not at all," chorused the friends.

"All right then," said the old gentleman, "First things first. Ozma and I will take Toto and Alexander to my work room, and there we will see what can be done about that dear dog's lost memory. The rest of you can watch my workers at their jobs in the meantime."

Later in his workroom, old St. Nick had put out mugs of chocolate for Ozma and himself on a crowded table next to a big chair, and separate dishes of water for Toto and Alexander. Then he placed Toto in the chair, saying, "OK, Toto. Now we'll get to the bottom of this. Just relax and take it easy. That's right." And Santa kept talking kind of soft and gentle to him until Toto was about three-quarters asleep.

By this time, around behind the chair and out of Toto's sight, he began doing a strange little dance, muttering some words that neither Alexander nor Ozma could understand. After a few minutes of dancing, the round old elf started moving slowly around the chair singing a little tune:

# Joom Discovered

"Whindaleara, whindalear.
Let his memory return
To this friend that is so dear,
So his mind again may learn
All that has not been so clear.
Windalurna, windalurn.

Stopping right in front of Toto, he looked deep into the little dog's eyes.

Toto, blinking, said hesitantly, "I, I don't feel any different."

"Yes, but how is your memory? asked Santa. "Do you remember any of your life in the Emerald City?"

"N-no," answered Toto slowly. "I don't seem to."

"Think about it. See if things do not seem to start clearing up."

Frowning a bit, the dog concentrated on thinking. He thought deeply. He thought and he thought. But nothing happened.

"No. I still do not remember any of my past, in the Emerald City nor anywhere."

"Oh. Oh," said Santa. "I was sure that would work. It is the best I could do. It should restore any lost memory."

"Suppose his memory was not actually lost," indicated Ozma. "Suppose it's all right there, but hidden behind a wall of magic."

"Umm. Yes. Yes. But I have no idea what to do about that."

"Nor I," added the little Queen.

They talked about it a bit and decided that if they

could not solve the problem of Toto's memory, they had better get to work on how to stop Joom.

"He's a one," declared Alexander. "I use t' know him pretty well when his name was Binkie, but as Joom, I feel like he's a complete stranger."

"What do you mean?" pressed Ozma. "What's this about Binkie?"

"Well, that there needs a bit of explainin'. An' th' truth is, I don' really understand it myself. Ya see, they're the same cat, but they ain't. Joom (as he is now) doesn't 'member much of what Binkie (as he use t' be) knew. Got me?"

"Not exactly," answered Santa Claus. "Do you mean that Binkie and Joom are the same cat on the outside, but inside they think differently?"

"Yeah," replied Alexander, "this Joom jus' ain't the same cat Binkie was — even if he does have the same body. An' I can't understand it at all. What's become of the real Binkie? Will we ever see him again? Joom can bounce back an' forth between Binkie's body an' his own but where's Binkie?" Almost in tears, Alexander finished, "He's never there at all anymore!"

Amazed that such a tough cat should have such tender feelings, the others began reassuring him. Before long he was ready to resume his story.

"Ya see, Binkie had gone aboard a fishin' boat with Merle for an early sea journey this spring."

Holding up her hand, Ozma, asked, "Who's Merle?"

"Just a tramp along the waterfront. He especially liked Binkie. Anyway, they was too early, an' got caught

# Joom Discovered

in a late storm—hit 'em hard and unexpected. Their boat broke up an' some of the people were rescued, but no one bothered t' look for a stray cat, an' Merle was not among the rescured, either. So we thought sure that was the end o' Binkie and Merle, but all a sudden Binkie showed up on the waterfront again three weeks ago, tryin' t' round up all the toughest cats he could find. O' course that included me.

"Well, he got quite a gang of us t'gether an' ya can imagine our su'prise when wham! Here we were in the Land of Oz. He told us the journey'd be pretty sudden, but none of us knew such a thing t' be possible.

"He told us t' pretend that we'd always lived in Oz, an' he put each of us in charge of a section of Oz cats — 'cept f'r me an' Honey Cat. Honey Cat he wanted t' be his mouthpiece, an' me, he wanted me t' be your guard, Toto."

"Hah!" laughed the dog, placing his front paws on the arm of the chair and leaning over toward his feline friend. "You sure did a good job of that! Why didn't he send you with me in the wagon with the Holder?"

"He thought that wise ol' guy'd be 'nuff of a guard. But I guess ya never can tell."

At this, Ozma interrupted, "The Holder? Why is he mixed up in this?"

"I dunno. Joom jus' said as he could keep anythin' all tied up."

"Hmm. Yes," interjected Mr. Claus as he took a drink from his mug while he perused his autofile. "My records show that security is his business, and that he never

175

takes sides. Give him something he can use, and he'll guard anything, anything at all."

"He seems to know all the angles," commented the Queen as she picked Toto up in her arms. "But what was the importance of putting a guard on Toto?"

"Well, ya see, Joom fig'red that Toto should be captured an' held f'r ransom. He knew that ya'd do practically anything t' get Dorothy's little dog back safe. His army o' cats oughta been enough, but just in case ya didn't yield, ya'd never see Toto again."

"Oh, how terrible!" exclaimed Ozma.

"The fiend!" muttered Santa Claus.

"Quite a plan," continued Ozma. "But now, tell us more about Binkie and Joom. How did this confusion of beings happen?"

As he jumped up into the chair where Toto had been, Alexander answered, "Well, that's hard t' explain. I don' understand it myself, but what he said was that when he fell inta the water he caught an' clung t' a piece o' wood barely big enough t' float him. He was on it no tellin' how long 'cause he passed out. When he came to he could do magic."

Ozma stopped him with a hand on his shoulder, "The magic just came to him out of nowhere?"

Pushing against her hand, he purred for a moment, then said, "He didn't seem t' have any explanation for it at all. And strangely, he knew 'bout this big Spelling Bee. Binkie did, and he'd never been in Oz. Never."

"What's a Spelling Bee?" asked Ozma. Then, using one hand to arrange her hair back from her brow, she

# Joom Discovered

added, "But I suspect I have an idea."

"Yup. He's a big bee that can cast about any spell ya could think of. So he looked him up an' had him put a Counter-Spell on all the cats 'cept for us from Seattle, an he put it on Toto an' hi'self, too."

"A Counter-Spell!" exclaimed Ozma with a little jump. "That is a spell against all other spells and magic of every kind. Why that explains everything. That is why none of our magic could locate Toto and why the Magic Book had nothing to say about Joom and the cats. No magic could reach them in any way!"

There was silence for a moment while the truth sunk in for everyone. Suddenly, the Queen spoke again, "And that means that none of Glinda's magical defenses will work at all. She is just as vulnerable as was the Emerald City. I must warn her at once and then gather the magic workers I was supposed to. Maybe one of them will have a means of dispelling the Counter-Spell."

"Ho, now," cautioned Santa as he put a hand on Ozma's shoulder. "Not so fast. We have other visitors arriving that will be more help than all the other magic workers in Oz. As for warning Glinda, I will send Black Peter in the sleigh pulled by Dancer. He will be there and back in a flash."

Ozma nodded her head, saying, "That sounds good, but what do you know about this Joom?"

"Ah," replied Santa. "That is a good question. He is a mystery to me. There was no such person until just a few weeks ago. He appeared in a cave on a deserted shoreline of the Nonestic Ocean and he changes back and forth between a man and a cat. He has organized a revolt of the cats of Oz. He seems to be a pretty bad character. That's about it."

As Santa led the way back to the others, he could be heard to mutter, "You never know what's going to happen next."

# Chapter 19

# Mysteries Resolved

oon after leaving Jack Pumpkinhead's, Sir Hokus had worried a bit and then broke the silence, saying, "I doth hope we reacheth the Emerald City afore those varlet cats."

When in response the Cowardly Lion quickened his pace, Dorothy warned, "But do be careful Lion. You don't want to wear yourself out so you can't run at all."

With that everyone settled into quietness except for a brief mumbling from the Spelling Bee flying overhead. Then, in less than an hour, the Cowardly Lion skidded to a stop as he came to the top of a hill and the four could see the spires of the Emerald City ahead of them.

"Hey! Wh-wh-at's going on here?" he exclaimed. "How c-c-could we be at the Emerald C-c-city already? I-it isn't possible. I have n-n-never run that fast b-b-before! Not even the S-s-sawhorse can run that f-fast. S-s-something is v-v-very wrong!"

At that the Spelling Bee blushed a bit and tried to explain: "Ah, well, you see … Dear me, I suppose I should have said something about that. But, you know, you were all so concerned with getting here quickly. So

# Toto and the Cats of Oz

… well, ah … I just kind of quietly worked a speed spell on the Lion. I hope you do not mind too much."

Shaking a bit the Lion said, "I-I guess that's all right." Then with a little laugh, he added, "It … well, it has been fun for a change. Maybe I could even win a race with the Sawhorse."

"Ahem now, I would be glad to take that spell off if you want me to. You know, whatever spell can be devised, my Dis-Spell can break it."

"No-o," responded Dorothy, "If things are not right in the Emerald City, we may be very glad for that extra speed. Let's leave it be for awhile."

It did not take long for them to find out just how not right things were. As they approached the West Gate, a large crowd of cats poured out of it.

"They look m-m-mean," declared the Cowardly Lion. "Do you want me to clear a path through them?"

"Oh no, dear Lion," Dorothy replied, "it looks like we're already too late to warn the Emerald City, so we had better head for Glinda's."

By this time the unruly mob of cats was almost upon them, but the newfound speed of the Cowardly Lion left the lesser felines far behind in an instant as he swung around the great City to reach the South Road to Glinda's Palace.

Yet again, before long, they faced another crowd of cats coming toward them from the south. There were several hundred of them of all types and varieties, spreading across the road and for twenty feet or so on each side of it. These were basically the same cats that

# Mysteries Resolved

had briefly captured Ozma's party. Now, a day later, and with their numbers greatly increased, they were doubly frustrated, having lost their regal captive and having run so hard in a fruitless chase. They were angry and ready for some sort of revenge. So, when they caught sight of our friends, they immediately started running toward them, howling and screeching.

Shaking like a leaf in a cyclone, the Cowardly Lion prepared to stand his ground while Sir Hokus, drawing his sword as he leapt from the saddle, cried out, "For honor and Princess Dorothy!"

"Stop! Stop!" called the Spelling Bee to his new friends. Buzzing excitedly, he reminded them that despite their best efforts, with so many cats attacking, Dorothy would surely get seriously hurt, whereas the Lion could easily outrun anything in the whole Land of Oz. Realizing that again, flight would be wiser than a fight, the brave knight remounted and away they sped, this time across the fields to the east.

Pausing to look back from a green hilltop and seeing no cats in sight, the Lion growled, "We are well rid of them although I would have swatted them to left and right except for the danger to Dorothy."

"I too, would gladly have stayed our journey for the joy of battle, save for the peril to M'Lady Dorothy!" exclaimed Sir Hokus of Pokes.

"Hush now," said Dorothy. "I have been thinking. The cats will probably be on all the main roads. So, to avoid them, we should stick to wild areas as much as possible," and gesturing to the south, she continued, "which should

# Toto and the Cats of Oz

mean going right through those mountains to Glinda's."

"B-but look how b-b-big those mountains are," stammered the Cowardly Lion. "N-no telling what dangers m-m-might lurk there!"

"Maybe none," said the Spelling Bee, "and we know what dangers lie on the road."

"Yes, and those cats are kind of scary to me," put in Dorothy.

"It is settled then," declared the Cowardly Lion, "for I certainly would not want to take anyone on a route that scared them. To the mountains!"

As they started, Dorothy pointed into the mountains and said, "Now do not worry my brave old friend. See that low spot? Just head for it. I have been here before and that will lead us to an easy route through, as well as to an old friend."

Sure enough, in less than an hour they had topped the last mountain pass and found themselves looking down as had the others, upon Christmas Valley.

Dorothy said, "Here we are!"

"Yea, verily," replied Sir Hokus, "but what delightful Alpine village does my eye behold down there?"

"Christmas Valley."

"I should have known," responded the Cowardly Lion. "This is a different pass from the one we came through nine years ago, but of course, this is where you'd expect to find Santa's Workshop. That's Viridian Mountain towering above this pass, and Scarlet Mountain across the way there—green and red—exactly the right place for Santa Claus."

182

# Mysteries Resolved

They hurried on down the slope toward the quaint little town, arriving at the same familiar inn where the others were already settled. Santa met them at the door, where they were greeted by friends and ushered into the Great Fireplace Room and their friends. On the one hand, Dorothy, Sir Hokus and the Cowardly Lion were greeted as old friends by Ozma, Uncle Henry, Scraps and the Sawhorse, but the latter were very curious about the Spelling Bee, while the former wondered what in the world a cat was doing amongst them.. Finally both greetings and explanations were completed, and elves began bringing refreshments for them all.

As they settled down to enjoy these treats, it was obvious that Dorothy was ill at ease. So it was not long before Santa said, "Yes Dorothy, I know. You are worried about Toto, aren't you?"

"Why yes, but how did you know?"

"Do you forget that it is my business to know what girls and boys are doing?"

"I guess that is right," responded Dorothy.

"Forsooth, and canst thou tell us in like manner of the doings of ye little dogs as well?" queried the metel-clad Hokus.

"Ho, ho, ho! Well put, Sir Knight. Easily done, for it so happens that Toto is right here in this very building."

"Here? ... In this building? ... Where? ... Take us to him ... Bring him here ..." The responses tumbled out upon one another until finally Santa said, "Ho now. He will be with us in a moment." And no one had taken more than two breaths before Toto really did trot through the archway into the Great Fireplace Room. With a cry of joy, Dorothy ran to him and swept him up in her arms.

"Oh Toto, Toto! I was so worried about you!" she sobbed with tears streaming from her face. "But here you are, and everything is all right again."

Toto responded by licking his mistress's face as any dog would, but he confessed later that, although it seemed a natural enough thing to do, at the time, he certainly had no idea who that sweet little girl was.

After a few minutes, Dorothy said, "It is so amazing, Santa, how you know what everyone is doing all the time. Isn't it hard to keep track of all that?"

"Oh, indeed it is. It's not the finding out. After all, I'm

*"Oh Toto, Toto! I was so worried about you!" she sobbed.*

# Mysteries Resolved

the one that directed Glinda in the magic to construct her Magic Book of Records and Ozma's Magic Picture. But the keeping track? That is the problem. All I can say is, it took long years of practice and discipline. And now, in recent years, I have computers to store it all.

"Toto was a problem though. Because of the Counter-Spell, I did not know it was him. All I knew was that a cat named Alexander was coming this way and kept talking to some unseen and unrecorded presence. It was not until they reached the first trees in Christmas Valley that one of the wood nymphs on duty there brought me the news, while I was talking to Ozma's party, that Alexander was accompanied by Toto."

"Well now," drawled Uncle Henry, "how come the Spelling Bee's spell kept you from knowing about Toto, but it didn't keep you from knowing about Alexander?"

While the Spelling Bee cleared his throat to speak, Alexander piped up, "That's easy. He didn't put the spell on me. Joom didn't have any o' us cats from America put under th' spell, 'cause he wanted us t' be able t' use magic – said he had various magic tools he'd want us t' use, but that anyone protected from magic by the Counter-Spell couldn't use magic at all."

"That is exactly right. Yes, it is," added the Spelling Bee. "It is a very powerful spell, and Joom, protected by it, is also prevented from using any magic. I guess you might say he was more concerned about protecting himself than preserving his powers. Yes, indeed."

Up to now Ozma had remained quietly at the edge of the group. Now she stepped quickly forward to

185

the center. Standing near the Spelling Bee, she said, "Speaking of the Counter-Spell, I think it is about time we were removing it from Toto." And looking right at the big Bee, she continued, "I believe you have the power to do that."

"Why, ah, yes, yes," stammered the embarrassed Bee, "that I can, er, ah, do. Yes, yes indeed," adding rather bashfully, "I am so ashamed of myself, but I was tricked into it. But then, he couldn't have tricked me if I hadn't been so vain. I am so very sorry, yes sorry. Oh, Queen Ozma, let me tell you the whole story. Oh! that terrible cat!"

"Yes," answered the Queen as she sat down, "I think you do have some explaining to do. Go ahead."

So, once more, the Bee told his story, now for all to hear. When he was finished, Ozma said, "Your magic has been responsible for a great deal of trouble, but it is clear that, far from meaning any harm, you had only meant to help cats you believed to be in danger. That is why we have outlawed the use of magic in our land. Even the best of people can cause unintended mischief. Now, I think we can make use of your magic to undo the trouble it has created."

With these words, she arose from the chair in which she sat and, again, she and Santa Claus took Toto and Alexander to Santa's office. However, this time the Spelling Bee and Dorothy went with them. Once Toto was settled in the big chair, the Bee started wiggling his antennae and waving both sets of arms as he chanted the same words the others had heard that morning at

# Mysteries Resolved

Jack Pumpkinhead's house:

"Away and gone, the spell is wrong.
Let what's been done be now undone."

"Is that all there is to it?" asked Alexander.

Without waiting, Santa once more began the elves' dance and chant for the restoration of memory. After the last words had died away there was a moment of complete silence. Then Toto jumped up, barked several times, and cried out, "I remember it all now! I remember it all! Dorothy, my dear Dorothy, and Ozma, Santa Claus, Alexander, and even the big Bee from that Winkie meadow. I remember Joom and his terrible plans, and I remember seeing him as a very ugly person and everything!"

With that he began barking again and tearing around the office as fast as he could run. His joyful friends kept trying to pat him as he dashed by. All were overjoyed, not only to have him back among them, but especially because now his memory had been restored.

# Chapter 20

# Return to
# the Ruby Castle

ll the elves and knooks and ryls and nymphs and fairies that were not needed elsewhere had gathered in the Great Fireplace Room with Dorothy's five friends. All waited on the return of Toto, half expectant that his memory would be restored, half afraid that it would not be.

Sir Hokus kept pacing up and down the great room, while the Cowardly Lion lounged contentedly on the hearth before the big fire. Not far from the Lion, but far enough to be safe from those dangerous sparks from the fireplace, Scraps sat upon the back of the Wooden Sawhorse, holding lively conversation with anyone who happened near her. Uncle Henry was quieter, but he too, was in frequent, if more serious, conversation with Santa's helpers.

Suddenly, all fell silent as Toto and Dorothy returned to the room, followed by the Spelling Bee, Ozma, Alexander and Santa Claus.

Toto was no more than through the door when he barked out, "I'm cured! I remember everything!"

As if in a single voice, a great shout of "Hurray!" went

# Return to the Ruby Castle

up from all those gathered in the room. Then a hubbub of voices broke loose as everyone was congratulating Toto, and exclaiming over the powers of the Spelling Bee, and thanking Santa Claus and Ozma, and asking Dorothy how she felt and telling each other, "Isn't it wonderful?"

Finally Santa Claus raised his hands for silence and said, "We thought we would wait to hear Toto's story until we could all be together again. So let us all be silent and hear what he has been through during the last few days."

With such a crowd waiting to hear him, Toto felt more than a little self-conscious at first. He started talking rather hesitantly, but soon warmed to their interest in the subject and forgot about his nervousness.

He began by briefly explaining the story of Joom-Binkie to all who had not already heard it. He pointed out that the vagabond cat's singing was not of the best quality, but he did have a lot of good stories to tell.

"Even so," said Toto, "I really had little to do with him until one day, nearly a week ago, when I was exploring the back part of the Royal Gardens. Far from the usual paths, I caught a fresh scent of Joom. With a mild kind of interest, I followed his spoor until it led me right into Ozma's private Garden of Magic."

"Where, for crying out loud" interrupted Scraps, "she grows all kinds of magical herbs that could be dangerous in the wrong hands."

"What in tarnation was he doing in there?" wondered Uncle Henry.

"Exactly," answered the little black dog. "Anxiety,

189

now, was added to my curiosity as I followed him with the utmost caution.

"When I did find him, he was leaning on that long staff of his, stamping his hind feet, repeatin 'Joom,' 'Joom,' 'Joom,' each time a little louder as he gradually changed into a most repulsive looking man — a long, creased face with big round ears and eyes that shone with a strange light, accenting their exaggerated size. He was all too strange and sinister looking.

As the others uttered "Ohs," and "Ahs," Alexander joined in with, "That's right. That's jus' the way he'd do it. Whichever form he was in, he'd pronounce the name o' the other three times, lean on that rod, stamp his feet

*" . . . he changed into a most repulsive looking man . . ."*

marvel t' behold. An' he was always very careful that no one but us cats from America ever saw him make that change 'cept for that one time when he wanted Toto to see his transformation."

"Yes," continued Toto. "You can imagine how startled I was when I saw that transition from cat to man. I just stood and stared. In that moment he tossed some glistening powders upon me, and, shouting some strange words, he tapped me with his long stick. Suddenly, I could not remember a thing. In a few moments I could not even remember that that had happened, and from then to now I have been confused and without memory. I would do whatever he wanted me to just because I did not know what else to do."

With that a murmur of voices interrupted: "Oh my! ... How sad! ... Poor Toto!"

Alexander took the opportunity to say, "Joom planned it that way. He wanted t' capture ya t' hold ya as a hostage, jus' t' be sure that Ozma would cooperate with him. Boy, I'll bet he's hoppin' mad now that you've escaped!" Then he added, "Go ahead. Tell 'em 'bout that."

"Luckily, the Queen of the Field Mice was in the weeds when Joom had the Holder pack me into his wagon to take to his Holding. So she sent four of her mice along to chew me loose."

"Chew you loose?" queried Dorothy.

"Yes. They were to chew through the ropes holding my cage in place so it could bounce out of the wagon, and that is exactly what happened. I guess the impact of my cage hitting the ground jolted some of the effect of Joom's magic out of me. At least, now I could remember what was going on, even though I still could not recall anything that had happened before I fell out of the Holder's wagon.

"Joom's magic must not be so very good then," remarked Ozma, "for, ordinarily, a mere bump will not knock loose the effects of magic."

"Maybe in all that time he'd disappeared he had not been able to use any magic, and he was rusty," commented Santa.

"I suppose," answered the little Princess. "In any case, we have interrupted. Please continue, Toto."

As they quieted, the dog resumed his story, recalling those several days of complete confusion. Now he could remember everything that had been happening. There was the trip west to the Spelling Bee where both he and Joom, as a cat, were put under the Counter-Spell so no more magic could affect them or even reveal their whereabouts.

Finally his story was complete and everyone felt that all the mysteries had been unraveled. All that remained was for the Spelling Bee to remove his Counter-Spell from Joom and his army. That would put a stop to all this trouble, and could not be done until they actually faced Joom.

Now, there was nothing more to do. Evening had come, so Santa Claus took them in to a big feast. After a long dinner, and a couple of stories of the old days from Old St. Nick and Henry, everyone went off to bed.

# Return to the Ruby Castle

The next morning they were all up early for breakfast, and off to the south on the trip to Glinda's. This time the Cowardly Lion only had Sir Hokus to carry, for Dorothy was riding in Santa's sleigh so she could hold Toto on her lap. Also in the sleigh, Alexander cuddled between Henry and Scraps, while the Spelling Bee flew along side. Everyone was traveling at a tremendous speed, so much so that the Sawhorse, with Ozma on his back, was actually a bit upset because the reindeer and the Lion were matching his own great speed.

"Don't pout so," said Ozma. "The Spelling Bee will take his Speed Spell off the Lion and himself as soon as the Revolution of the Cats has been stopped, and then you will once more be the fastest creature around."

"Except for Santa's reindeer," grumbled the Sawhorse.

"But they are different," countered Dorothy. "If they could not go faster than light, we would never get our Christmas presents. Now you would not want that to happen, would you?"

The Sawhorse had just begun to answer when he stopped with his mouth wide open. Everyone else stopped and stared as well, for where the Spelling Bee had been an instant before, there was now, nothing! He had completely and instantaneously disappeared.

Scraps was the first to speak with the simple question, "Where'd he go?"

The Cowardly Lion began shaking so hard that Sir Hokus had to hold on for dear life, and all began murmuring.

Ozma held up her hand for silence and then said, "I

believe that Joom has found us in my Magic Picture and used the Magic Belt to spirit the Spelling Bee away for fear he might undo that wicked cat's plans."

"But," protested Sir Hokus, "how could that be? Ye great Bee hath averred that any who art protected by ye Counter-Spell cans't in no wise worketh any magic."

"That's an easy one," answered Alexander. "Remember, Joom knew about that, an' didn't never take any o' us cats from America t' the Spellin' Bee, so we ain't pertected from magic. But that suits him OK, 'cause then we can make magic equipment work. So ol' Joom probably jus' had Honey Cat use the Magic Picture an' the Magic Belt under his direction. Simple, hunh?"

"Simple, but dangerous for us," snorted the Wooden Sawhorse.

With that everyone fell to discussing the disasters that might soon overcome the land. Some said this and some said that. They worried a bit this way and that way. What could they do to save the Land of Oz from Joom's evil intent?

Finally, Ozma asked for quiet again, saying, "Let us not worry too much. Glinda is bringing together the greatest assembly of magic workers that Oz has ever seen. Surely together, we will be able to defeat Joom, and in the process we will find the Spelling Bee and bring him back in time to help."

"Of course," cried Scraps. "To horse and away to Glinda's!"

Pausing only long enough for everyone to get comfortably seated again, they were soon off at top speed.

# Return to the Ruby Castle

This time the Sawhorse was not the least bit disturbed that the Cowardly Lion could match his speed. In fact, he was glad he did not have to wait on the others, for, like everyone else, his only concern was reaching Glinda's as quickly as possible.

With all this speed, it took hardly half an hour more for them to reach their destination, where Glinda met them at the gate.

As they dismounted, she told them how she had followed their adventures in the Great Book of Records. Of course, Dancer had already brought the news that Joom was the conqueror of the Emerald City and that a Counter-Spell prevented all magic from having any effect on him and his cats. Santa had also sent with him the news of the arrival of the Spelling Bee, who alone could remove the Spell. Now, having just read of the disappearance of that all important Bee, she was well aware of the trouble this meant for all of them.

But she continued, as she led them toward her conference room, "There is good news, too. Many of the finest magic workers in the world have gathered here," and she proceeded to name them.

When she mentioned Reera the Red, Uncle Henry interrupted, saying, "I thought she never put her finger's into other people's pie."

"That is true." replied Ozma. "Ordinarily she stays to herself in her Gillikin cottage, amusing herself with her Yookoohoo magic, but refusing to use it either to help or to harm anyone else." Then, speaking to Glinda, she asked, "How did you ever convince her to help us?"

195

# Toto and the Cats of Oz

"I didn't," replied the Good Sorceress. "She volunteered. Her own red cat has disappeared and she wants to get it back."

At this Toto barked out a little dog laugh and said, "I am sure her cat is on the way here right now — along with a million others."

"I am afraid you are right," answered Ozma, "but Reera may be the very one who can pierce the barrier of the Counter-Spell."

"How could that be?" asked Uncle Henry.

At the same time, Alexander said, "That Counter-Spell can't be broken!"

"True," replied Glinda, "but Ozma is right. Yookoohoo magic is an extremely powerful means of transformation, so Reera may be able to do what none of the rest of us could. We have to see if she can transform one spell into another. Maybe she can do that to the Counter-Spell."

"Wheow," whistled Uncle Henry. "That would be some trick."

By this time, they had reached their destination: Glinda's Conference Room. Spread out around them was a great room hung with rich red drapes. Coming to the large mahogany tables, the various magic workers were already being seated, and with them, Glinda's chief lieutenants.

The young women in Glinda's Palace Guard were gathered from all corners of Oz, and each of them was lovely to look upon, but it was a loveliness born more of honest character than of physical beauty. To be chosen to serve at Glinda's Palace was the greatest honor that

# Return to the Ruby Castle

could come to a young lady in the Land of Oz, and each of them was proud to have the opportunity to work with the ageless sorceress who seemed as young as they. All wore identical red uniforms—identical, except for the facing of the pleats of their skirts. These were colored to denote the country that each girl called her home—blue for a Munchkin lass, yellow for both of the girls from the Winkie Country, solid red for two Quadlings, purple for Teriane, who was a Gillikin, and green for one young girl from the Emerald City.

With the room now filled, Ozma quickly told them all of Joom and his conquest of, not only the Emerald City, but also much of the rest of Oz. She told, too, of the Spelling Bee, his Counter-Spell protecting the cats from all magic, the importance of him in cancelling that Spell, and of his sudden disappearance.

Many opinions were voiced as to how best to meet the perils they faced, but at last it was up to Ozma to give the necessary orders. Sir Hokus would organize the defenders of the palace. Uncle Henry, Toto and Alexander would work as an inspection team to make certain there was not even the smallest crack for the tiniest kitten to creep through the walls.

Finishing her instructions to everyone else, one might think that the little Queen was being childish, for she went off to a private room, taking two stuffed bears with her. However, these were two very special bears. One was a full sized, very much alive stuffed bear known as the Lavender Bear, so called because that was the color of his fur. He carried with him an apparently lifeless one named Pink Pinkerton, and yes, his fur was a beautiful shade of pink. Together, these two had special magic for finding lost things which had been very helpful to Ozma in the past.

Once inside the room, she addressed the Lavender Bear, who was also the King of Bear Center, "Let us begin by seeing the Spelling Bee."

Taking out a little wand which looked like silver but was not, he waved it three times, and immediately, right in front of them, they could see the image of the Spelling Bee sleeping soundly on a big flat bed.

"He looks safe enough," remarked the big bear.

"But," asked the little Queen, with a puckering of her brow, "where is he?"

"For that we will seek Pink Pinkerton's advice." Even as the Princess had asked, the King of Bear Center had been picking up his little bear and turning a crank that protruded from its side. All the bears of Bear Center are stuffed bears in all colors, sizes and shapes, but this is the only one that behaves like a stuffed bear. All the others are as alive as you or me, but Pink Pinkerton never shows any sign of life until that handle is cranked. Then, for a short time, he can move and talk. And when he talks, he can answer any question put to him about anything that has already happened. And the answer he gives is always absolutely truthful. No one knows why he can do this, but he always works just this way.

As soon as his crank was turned, the little one responded, as was his habit, stiffly turning his head from side to side, and crying out in a shrill little voice, "Hurrah

# Return to the Ruby Castle

for the King of Bear Center."

Ozma clapped her hands at this, while the big bear started a line of questions: "Tell us where they have put the Spelling Bee."

"In a bed."

"Yes. We know that, but where is that bed?"

"It is in a house."

"A house in what town?"

"In the town of Pokes."

"Hurrah for Pink Pinkerton of Bear Center," laughed Ozma, then she looked more serious as the big lavender bear pointed out, "But if that is where he is, he will just sleep and sleep and sleep and never be able to get out of there."

"You're right, of course, so I suppose we should see just where he is in Pokes. Can you do that for us King?"

"Of course I can," he answered as he again waved his wand three times, and again they saw the giant Bee, but this time they were looking through a widow into a particular house.

"OK. Now let us see where that house is in the town of Pokes."

Another three waves of the big lavender bear's wand and the view slowly drew back so that they could see the house's location in the town.

Grabbing the big bear by his shoulders, Princess Ozma declared, "Now I think we are ready to dispatch someone to retrieve him."

"Who should that be?" asked the King.

"You know what to look for, so you should be one.

# Toto and the Cats of Oz

The Chief Poker of Pokes might be more reasonable in dealing with fellow rulers from the Winkie Country. Then, since people who go to Pokes tend to get sleepy, I'll find someone who has an anti-sleep charm to go with you."

It took only a few minutes to find that Queen Zixi had just such a charm. Then Ozma said, "For fast service we need to find the Wooden Sawhorse to carry you."

It took a little longer to find the Sawhorse, but they finally found him following behind, Toto, Alexander and Uncle Henry, checking to be sure they were not missing any possible cat holes. Of course, they were not, but as he said, "You just can't be too careful."

When they explained this new mission to him, his immediate response was to rear back saying, "Let us not be too hasty. I am told that everyone who goes into Pokes goes to sleep forever."

"Never fear," answered Gloma, "I have an anti-drowse spell that will keep us awake, no matter what."

"I hope so," grumbled the wooden steed.

"Then we should be off," declared the Lavender King.

"Don't you mean 'on?'" demanded the Sawhorse, stamping his feet.

"All right," laughed the Black Queen, "'On' we will get," and she hopped in place on his back.

The King of Bear Center quickly joined her and the next thing they knew they were off — off on their journey, that is, with the promise to be back by mid-afternoon.

# Chapter 21

# The Defense of the Castle

ension ran through the defenders of the Ruby Castle like static electricity, needing only one touch to set it off. Almost that touch came in the form of one bedraggled and dust-covered cat that suddenly appeared running down the castle's main hall.

"They have broken through," wailed the Cowardly Lion as, shaking in every hair of his body, he prepared to jump upon the oncoming cat.

"Wait, wait." cried Glinda. "Puss! Is that really you? What on Ozeria has happened?"

"I have been running as fast as I could both night and day," gasped the new arrival, "and have just come in through my secret entrance. But hurry now! It is hidden by magic and that will not detain those cats at all."

"Yes. Yes," declared Glinda. "Someone must seal it off before the other cats find it. Once they do, all will be over, for there is nothing our magic can do against them. Uncle Henry, Teriane …"

With no need to speak, just a nod, they were off, taking additional helpers with them.

# Toto and the Cats of Oz

To the others, Glinda explained that her cat's secret entrance was guarded by magic so powerful that none other than Puss could use it. But, Joom's cats, invulnerable to magic, could easily see it and pass right through it. Then, turning again to Puss, she exclaimed, "You look terrible! Are you all right?"

"I guess so," replied the cat. "I can still move, but I'd sure like to have a good can of tuna and a warm comfortable spot to sleep."

"I'm off to the kitchen," said Golnora, one of the Girl Guards with the purple facing of a Gillikin in her skirt, nodding to Glinda as she hurried on her way.

The large, dark red cat continued, "While I'm waiting, I'll tell you about my strange experience. It all began with a rally of cats. A couple I know in a neighboring village came by to invite me to go with them. I did. It sounded like fun: free milk, cats from all over, caterwauling contests and some of the top cat singers of Oz. If we had known the real purpose, we would never have gone.

"There was this strange and evil cat named Joom behind it all. He had been going around holding secret cat rallies and stirring up cats all over Oz. Besides speaking briefly himself, he had a golden-tongued orator along named Honey Cat. Between them, they really whipped that crowd into a frenzy. I doubt if any of the cats ever thought they were not treated as equals by humans before they heard those two.

"Anyway, after listening for awhile, even I decided they had a point, but revolution! That was too much! However, I decided to go along just to keep an eye on things.

# The Defense of the Castle

"We were all taken to a meadow where a giant bee was to put a spell on us so that magic would have no effect upon us. I figured that whatever that scruffy cat wanted, I'd better do just the opposite, so I hid in a grove of trees and rejoined the cats after the casting was over. I was placed in a patrol headed about as far from here as possible — way up north beyond the Forest of Gugu. Pretty quickly, I decided that I had learned all I was going to and slipped away, headed here, pretending I was a special courier. Along the road, I found that the Emerald City had been taken and orders given to storm this key fortress of resistance. Well, you can guess that gave wings to my speed, and here I am, but only a little ahead of the others."

By this time, Golnora was back with two dishes, one of canned tuna and one of milk. While Puss turned to it, there was a flapping of wings announcing the arrival of the Dread Ravens:

"The bone. The bone. It glows.
All too much it shows
Magic 'gainst us grows,
For someone works your woes!"

"Thank you, my friends," replied Glinda. "Make haste, go to warn those who stand watch on the battlements and at the gates."

Then quickly, she gave orders to Golnora to bring all her magic workers together above the Main Gate. To the others she said, "We are well prepared. Uncle Henry's crew has us tightly sealed against any cats sneaking in, and the Magic Barrier that Ozma and I placed around this palace will certainly stop any magic this Joom may have his American cats try to use against us. So come. Let us go up to face him and his rebellious cats."

They were behind the battlements above the Front Gate before any of the cats had arrived, but Glinda's scouts had also come in, reporting that thousands of cats were approaching from all directions.

While they waited, Ozma said, "As we all know, the Spelling Bee's Counter-Spell protects these cats from the effects of magic. If the Bee were here, he would remove it and we could deal with them quickly, but the cats hold him captive, so we must do our best. Hopefully there is some flaw in the spell, a flaw that one of us can exploit to our own good."

Only moments more went by before the entire army of cats burst upon the castle, coming out of the wood from all sides, meowing and screeching. Right up to the walls they came like an incoming tide. But there, they stopped as waves wash against towering cliffs.

Upon the walls, the assortment of wizards, witches, magicians and sorceresses were busily at work trying to use their best magic against the cats. Oh, what a stench went up from the bubbling cauldrons, burning powders and smoking torches. Lightning flashed. The wind howled. Darkness came and went several times in the brief span of half an hour. But the cats were unaffected.

At the same time, Joom was busy with his own magical display. Of course, the Counter-Spell kept him

# The Defense of the Castle

from doing any of it himself, but he had the cats from America with him, hidden in the trees in the back ranks of the cats. He had them using the Magic Belt and his own Magic Stick commanding such things as the gates to open, the walls to fall, the people on the walls to freeze or for Dorothy to appear in the woods beside them. Naturally, none of this worked, for the mystical barrier placed by Glinda and Ozma was thoroughly effective against all forms of attack by magic. As a result, Joom's frustration was making his bad disposition steadily worse.

While most of the cats were trying to avoid Joom's ranting, on the walls of the palace, most of the magic workers had given up their attempts.

Now Reera the Red stepped to the fore. Though capable of appearing in a near infinite number of forms, she came as her natural self, handsomely dressed in a long red gown, with a belt of many jewels, a necklace of shining pearls and with her long, bright auburn hair billowing out behind her shoulders. As a Yookoohoo master of transformations, she was going to try to do exactly what Glinda had thought, change the Counter-Spell, itself, into some other kind of spell.

For a moment she stood, staring out upon the cats.

Then she began with a flourish, sweeping her hands out from behind her back as she transformed herself into a giant, snarling dog. The cats gasped and shuddered. Involuntary screams came from many of them. Standing on her hind legs, she pulled up from behind the parapet in front of her a dark gray flagon. Holding it between her two front paws, she poured it out into the air beyond the walls, where, instead of falling to the ground, it just floated as a pool of whitish liquid. Quickly, she pulled another flagon from behind the parapet and poured its contents onto that which already hovered there. Upon contact, the white liquids began to sparkle and mutated through pink to an ever deepening red, while Reera chanted:

> "Flowzin a gobbin,
> Dey bobbble ah ruhben
> Flowzin a gobbin,
> Dey bobble ah luben
> Sey marc, an hobbin,
> Dah foumble fornuben."

As she spoke, the sparkling liquid began to emit real sparks. Repeating the words, the sparks became more intense. On the third time through, steam began to rise from the surface of the suspended red pool, flowing back down over its edges. As it drifted down, it was wafted out as a fine, pinkish mist that enveloped the cats. In a few minutes the mist began to fade away. While it was doing so, Reera resumed her own shape, watched the fading mist until it was quite gone, and then raised her arms slowly from her sides, out in front of her, straining as though drawing invisible masses up into the air.

Nothing happened.

After a silence made long by the hope of all those waiting along the wall, Reera finally admitted, "My best was not good enough. Had it worked, they would have

# The Defense of the Castle

floated off the ground. That bit of magic can change the effect of any other known spell. And yet it failed. We cannot break through the Counter-Spell."

With that, she walked firmly back to stand beside Glinda. That Red Sorceress put her hand upon the Yookoohoo's arm, saying, "None of us could break through it, but neither can Joom's cats break down our walls, nor can his black arts break through our Magic Barrier."

Dorothy, standing on the other side of Glinda, commented, "I guess this means we are in kind of a stand-off."

Joom, however, was not going to be content with such a state of affairs. He had been staying hidden in the trees at the back of the crowd of cats. Like most that are cruel, he was a coward, willing to let the cats face danger as long as he was not involved. As Ozians, neither he nor they could be killed, but they could still suffer, and he didn't mind if they did, but he certainly was not going to put himself in harm's way.

The American cats were another matter. They could be killed, and since he had not put the Counter-Spell upon them, they could be attacked by magic, so he had kept them well hidden, even further back in the trees than where he was.

But now, with the magic over, it was time to talk. For this he had prepared Honey Cat. He sent for that tawny one and all the other American cats to join him in front of the palace gates. Hurrying himself, Joom soon reached a knoll right in front of where Ozma stood on the castle parapet.

# Toto and the Cats of Oz

"At last," he snarled, "we are face to face. In the name of all the cats of Oz, I declare your kingdom forfeit and establish in your place the reign of cats in the person of Joom the First, Emperor of Oz. Henceforth, all knees in the Land of Oz shall bend in homage to Joom the Great. Bow down!"

In chorus with his last exclamation, a loud shout went up from all the cats as they bent their front legs, touching their heads to the ground. Of course, none of the people or animals standing upon the wall moved in the least. As Joom peered around, viewing the bowing cats on one side, and the standing people on the other, his back arched in anger, and he cried out, "How dare you defy me!"

As the rest of the cats returned to standing on all fours, Honey Cat wended his way through them to the hillock where Joom stood. The self-styled emperor turned to him and with a smug grin upon his face, said, "OK, you tell it to them now."

The tawny cat stepped up beside his leader and began speaking. He could project his voice to be heard by all those along the parapet. Yet his tones were soft and modulated. He began in true oratorical fashion — saying much, without saying anything. Gradually he warmed up to his task until he was ready to go to the heart of the matter.

"You leave us no choice. We must revolt against your tyranny. From the beginning of time it has been here in Oz, as it is elsewhere. Cats are treated as creatures without rights. You expect us to do what you want us to do, but you never ask our opinions. You do not want to know that we have feelings and ideas.

"Yours is the story of all oppressors. Ours is the plight of all the oppressed. You expect us to come when you call, 'Here kitty, kitty.' And you expect us to go when you say 'scat!' You treat us as though we were some lower kind of creation. You like to hold us in your arms and pet us. And we purr because we like it, too. But you do it, not because we like it, but because *you* like it. You do not really care about us.

"And now, little Miss Ozma, hear the charges against you and against your Council and against all who advise you. Hear our grievances and tremble!"

Then, sitting back on his haunches, and alternating holding one forepaw and then the other aloft as he named off the complaints of his tribe, the beautiful cat began his list.

"The roll of your misdeeds against cats could be much longer, but we have summarized all your many crimes as follows:

"First: You gave us no part in the government of the Land of Oz. All the laws are for the benefit of human beings. None of the laws are made to benefit or protect cats.

"Second: We are not treated as equals. We are treated as subordinate beings.

"Third: No education is provided for cats. You have schools and training for human children. Why, even a bug has received a full education! But no thought is given to the raising of kittens.

# Toto and the Cats of Oz

"Fourth: Cats are given no part in the life of the community. Everything is planned for humans, nothing for cats.

"Fifth: You do not even let us eat at the same table with you. You feed us scraps and inferior food that you would not touch, and you deny us the fellowship of eating together.

"Sixth: You extend this barrier to all areas of life so that there can be no way in which we can share facilities with one another. In all activities of life we are separated and relegated to an inferior position.

"For these crimes against cats and for much more, we cry out for satisfaction. Because you have failed in your duty to rule the Land of Oz with fairness and justice for all, we demand your abdication in favor of Great Joom, the First!"

As Honey Cat stopped speaking and settled down upon all fours, the other cats echoed his words, "Abdicate! Abdicate!"

Their catcalls went on for about fifteen minutes, until finally, when Ozma raised her hands for silence, the cats were ready to be quiet and hear her.

"What your spokesman says has merit, but of course I am not going to abdicate under this kind of pressure. If the humans have been unfair to the cats we want to correct that. My friends and I go now to discuss it.

As the young Queen turned and walked away, the cats again started chanting, "Abdicate. Abdicate," but the fairness with which she spoke had somewhat subdued their voices.

210

# Chapter 22

# Honey Cat's Second Speech

hen Honey Cat had first appeared, even before he had started his speech, Alexander had quickly fallen into a conference with Toto. After a few minutes, Toto had gone over and whispered something to Dorothy and she had gone to whisper something in Glinda's ear. Then Glinda had gone down the stairs, not to appear again until after Honey Cat was done speaking. Now, as the chanting resumed and with Alexander standing beside her, with one hand, she drew a dark red fan from the folds of her, skirt and a bottle of liquid with the other. She flipped the fan open and closed several times while softly muttering words not heard by any others. Then, unstopping the bottle, she dipped the tip of the fan into it, and while whispering more magical words, she shook drops of the liquid toward Honey Cat. Instantly that golden cat sailed through the air and landed lightly right in front of Glinda.

He was still pawing at the air as Alexander exclaimed, "C'mon ya ol' reprobate. Le's go!" And off the two ran at top speed, with Alexander leading, down the stairs, right into Glinda's Throne Room.

# Toto and the Cats of Oz

There the big cat settled down into the soft, red, deep cushioned seat while Honey Cat stopped, surprised at its foot, and exclaimed, "Shouldn't we keep on running?"

"Naw," scoffed the other, whacking the cushion beside him with his paw. "We're safe enough. C'mon up here."

Jumping lightly into place, the golden cat asked, "When did they capture you?"

"Capture me? Ha, ha. Hasn't happened. I ran away."

"Why under the sun would you do a thing like that?"

"Aw, come off it, Honey Cat. Ya was there. Ya saw what the cats were doin' in the Emeral' city an' ol' Joom didn't give a fig about it. That was the end f'r me, an' it should'a been f'r you too. If the cats can't behave any better than that, they don't deserve t' rule any more than the humans."

Backing away a bit from his old friend, Honey Cat exclaimed, "What a thing to say!"

Scooting back himself, Alexander answered, "Now, ya need t' think about that. We came here t' help the cats get their freedom. Yet, when they get it, they act like tyrants themselves. Ya know I like a good fight as well as the next, but I'm never cruel. An' that's jus' what these cats became when Joom lead them inta the Emeral' City. I was disgusted and ashamed."

By this time Honey Cat had let himself move closer to the center of the pillow again and was listening thoughtfully to what his old friend was saying. From time to time he would interrupt and argue a bit, for he was fired up about his mission to save the cats. Alexander kept answering him with variations of, "Yeah, but the ends don't justify the means! It's no good usin' wicked ways t' help a good cause. That jus' defeats the good we'd like t' do." Then he would continue explaining what he had found out about the true personality of Joom, and the strangely unpleasant effect the human form of Joom had had upon both of them when first they met him as a human.

All that Alexander said was true, and bit by bit Honey Cat began to realize how badly Joom had mislead him. Finally it was clear to him, and he wasted only a few moments in bewailing his foolishness for being used by the evil magician for such bad purposes.

They trotted back out into the hallway. All was quiet in the direction of the Conference Room, but noises could be heard from the direction of the roof top, so they went in that direction.

In the meantime, Ozma and her friends had been discussing what to do about the demands of the cats. Most were fully incensed and counseled downright refusal. Some thought a compromise could be reached.

"But we cannot just give in to them," warned Reera. "Almost everyone but Glinda and I gave in to the Wicked Witches and look how long it took to overcome them!"

"Yea verily," exclaimed Sir Hokus, standing and brandishing his sword as he paced in front of the others, "hads't they come to us in peace, bearing a table of faults." —Swish!—"then of a surety could we grant their boon,"—Swish!—"but herein lies softness,"—Swish! —"if we let the violence of yon varlet cats decide our course of action,"—Swish and Stomp.

Nodding, Glinda asked, "Is a good cause to be set aside because it was unjustly begun? Do we not all agree, even as our good knight has implied, that their requests are justified?"

"But, it is the way they went about it," complained Reera, her saucy black eyes sparkling her defiance.

The Good Witch of the South, not wanting to be unkind to either of her friends, agreed quickly. "Of course, you are right. We do not want to approve the violence they have done. Then pausing and adjusting her white gown and her gleaming red hair, she continued more slowly, "But we do not want to make just as big a mistake as they did."

To the surprise of all, Toto hopped onto a chair and spoke in defense of the cats. "You all know that I was not well treated by them, but the felines do have a good point. It's not nearly as strong as what Joom tries to make it, but if we really listened, we could see that each of Honey Cat's points ring true. Laws are not made by the cats nor for them. They are not treated as equals. There are no schools for them. We do not include them in anything. Joom has convinced them that we have done this out of meanness when, really, it is just because we never thought of it before. More important, neither had the cats until Joom came along. Now that we have all thought about it, we ought to do something about it." He jerked his head up for emphasis, took a quick turn and lay down, all attention, on the chair.

Then Glinda stood up to summarize, "Some of you

# Honey Cat's Second Speech

have pointed out that it is wrong for the cats to use such violence to get what they want. That certainly is true, but is it any better for us to deny justice because we do not like what they have done?"

At this point, Ozma took to her feet, with her hands pressed firmly upon the table, and with equal firmness in her voice, declaring, "Glinda and Toto are right. We have not treated cats as equals, but we can from now on. We have nothing against them other than their bad behavior under Joom's tutelage. What they want is fair enough. It is Joom that has caused all the trouble. He has tried to use the cats' proper desires to serve his own selfish purpose of becoming Emperor of Oz.

"Yes, their requests are reasonable enough, and most of them will be granted. But abdicate? I will never do that under threat!"

"Hurray!" shouted her friends.

Amidst the hubbub, Ozma called for attention and the voices of those around her became quiet again. "Listen. I have a plan as to how we can accomplish these goals. Here is how it can be done."

For the next several minutes, she described what she had in mind.

Then she led her followers back up to the parapets where she found the cats in an even uglier mood than when she had left. Troubled by the absence of Honey Cat, Joom himself had stirred up their anger. This time they refused to listen to Ozma. They refused to talk to her. They just kept shouting, "Abdicate! Abdicate!"

As though things were not bad enough, now

something terrible came out of the woods. There could be no doubting the fearful purpose of the double column of twelve cats carrying a stout length of wood in a harness between them. Straight toward the castle they marched. Then came another headed for the same spot. As soon as they stood in their ordered lines in front of the palace doors, they began moving in time to the chant of "Abdicate! Abdicate!" Their rush forward made the beams of wood slung between them act as small battering rams.

Heavy doors such as guard most castles would not have been hurt by the blows from these little pieces of wood. However, Glinda's castle was protected by magic and her doors were decorative rather than strong. Since no magic could hold back the cats, by the time the third blow had struck a crack began to appear in one of the doors. With each successive blow, it grew and more cracks began to appear.

The cats cheered.

Within, Uncle Henry, Cap'n Bill and the Shaggy Man were hastily nailing large sheets of wood across the opening to back up the increasingly frail doors.

Suddenly, on the sixth charge of the cats, their little battering rams crashed against the doors with a loud sound of splintering wood.

The cats rejoiced with a cheer to rock the heavens. Then, a sudden silence fell upon them, for amazingly, it was not the door that had failed. It was the battering rams that had shattered.

The cats fell, stunned by this reversal of fortune. How

# Honey Cat's Second Speech

could it be? Then, bewildered, they began a nervous mewling among themselves.

Just then, Alexander and Honey Cat returned. Ozma spoke with them for a few moments, then turned and led the rest of her friends back down, inside the palace.

As the murmuring among the cats grew louder, Joom tried vainly to restore order. Suddenly Alexander and Honey Cat jumped up where they could be seen on the parapets. The confused mumbling that had started was replaced by cheers and cries of friendly greeting from the cats, glad to see their two heroes safe.

"Our problems are all taken care of," announced Alexander. "I'll let Honey Cat tell ya all about it."

As that golden cat stepped forward, a hush fell upon the crowd of cats, and he began speaking with soft modulation. "We, all of us, have just had a narrow escape. To know how close we came, you need to hear a story. It is a true story about a cat we all know very well.

"One day, about three weeks after a big storm, several of us were gathered on the docks back in America, mourning our good friend Binkie who had been lost at sea in that storm." He continued by swinging a forepaw to the right as he stared off in that direction, "Suddenly, who came strolling down the pier we sat upon, but Binkie himself." And now the emphasis of his words took on menace, "Only he told us we should call him, 'Joom.' He said …"

Abruptly, Joom cut in with a rasping voice, "Here now. What are you up to?"

"Why," replied Honey Cat in innocent tones, "I am

just telling our friends the true story of our great leader. Surely, you do not object to my telling them the truth." then, as if struck by a sudden thought, he added, "In fact, let me have all the cats from America come over here to stand with you, dear Joom, and if anything I say is untrue, they can stop me."

Joom did not miss the threat to him that would come from being surrounded by six stalwart, dock-brawling cats. But there was nothing he could do about it now.

As they gathered around the now nervous scraggly black cat, the beautiful tan one resumed, "This cat that all of us had known as Binkie, then tried to convince us that he had always been a great magician just pretending to be a cat — trying to convince us who had known him since he was a kitten!"

A variety of "oh's" and "ah's" interrupted the silky one at this point. Some were surprise, but many registered fear, and a few, even anger. Joom opened his mouth to speak, but as several of the American cats moved in closer to him, he said nothing.

Honey Cat continued, "Unable to convince us with words, he decided upon action. Leaning on a stick he carried in a harness and stomping his hind feet, Binkie-Who-Wanted-To-Be-Called-Joom, changed, right before our eyes, into an ugly, skinny, bent old man with a deeply lined face and funny round ears."

He was silent while his words sunk in. Then, scattered voices, hesitantly said, "Joom."

"Yes. A few of you have seen him in his angry fits. You know how mad he really is. All of you know how

# Honey Cat's Second Speech

he encouraged us to be cruel, saying, 'They deserve it,' 'They have treated us like crumbs long enough, 'Do it to them before they do it to us,' and with many other such false words.

"Can you imagine that? This faker who was really a human being himself, and not a cat at all, yet he would talk about 'us' as though he were a real cat. And all the time, all he wanted was to rule Oz."

Several times Joom had tried to interrupt, but in each case he would settle back when the six tough cats surrounding him would shoulder him a bit. Now he could restrain himself no longer. Quickly jumping clear of them, he cried out, "What are you doing? We are on the verge of success for all the cats. You will ruin it! I am a cat like the rest of you. He is telling you lies. Lies! All of it!" Then shouting even louder, "Storm the gates! Take that cat. He is under my personal condemnation. Tear him apart! Destroy the liar! I am Joom the Great, Emperor of Oz, and I can do whatever I want to do."

The cats were milling, murmuring, uncertain. Some were moving toward the gate, but in a disorganized way. Fruitlessly, Joom sank down in a heap with tears in his eyes, sobbing, "Destroy the liar."

"Let us see who is lying," declared Honey Cat as he turned toward the stairway, and Joom, shakily, arose.

From the shadows stepped forth Glinda, Scraps, the Cowardly Lion, Sir Hokus of Pokes, Dorothy and Toto. All the while, Joom stood, unmoving, his jaw set firmly and his tail snapping from side to side. Then, up the stairs, visible equally to the crowd of cats and the defenders of the palace, came Ozma. About her waist was the power-filled Magic Belt.

At the unexpected sight of this great instrument of magic, the last shred of Joom's bravado vanished. He thought he still had this trump safe in the woods with his own cats. What he did not know was that when Honey Cat had called the American cats to guard the wicked cat, they had left it behind them in the woods and the Dread Ravens had immediately swooped down and retrieved it for Ozma.

The young Queen now placed her hands upon the Belt and suddenly Joom was floating swiftly through the air to land in her now outstretched arms.

Spitting and trying to twist to scratch her, Joom quavered, "How did you get that Belt? I'll never be Emperor now. We cats are forever lost."

"You call yourself a *cat*? We shall see," said the Princess as, with one hand she placed him on the parapet in front of her, and with the other, touched the Magic Belt, calling out loud and clear, "Let Joom appear in his natural form."

Instantly, the angry cat disappeared, to be replaced by an ugly, little old man.

A gasp went up from the crowd of cats and voices calling out, "He has tricked us. He has tricked us all!"

In the confusion, that evil magician tried to run away, but as he turned one way, he faced the open mouth of the Cowardly Lion who just happened to be yawning at that moment. Turning the other way, he faced the drawn sword of Sir Hokus who quietly said, "Dost thou wishest

# Honey Cat's Second Speech

to be spitted or swallowed?"

Seeing he had no way out, Joom just stood there, slightly stooped, his face contorted in anger so that his teeth showed. The lines of his face almost glowed. His eyes behind thick glasses looked like coals of fire as he complained, "You had no right. This is not fair. How could you possibly break through the Counter-Spell?"

In answer, those around Ozma moved aside and out stepped the Spelling Bee.

"Ah," he hummed, "so you thought you could trick the bumbling old Bee, hmmm? Yes. Yes. But, twice now these good friends have released me from your little, ahem, tricks. Most recently, they brought me back just in time to catch you trying to break down the gates. Um, yes indeed. As soon as I saw what was afoot, I took the Counter-Spell off you and the cats, so, a-h-h yes, that made the magic in Glinda's doors effective against them. So, of course, hmmm, yes, their battering rams broke. Ah hah, and now here you are. Ah yes. I believe this puts an end to all your evil plans."

# Chapter 23

# The Punishment of Joom

fter the Spelling Bee had finished talking, Joom made some quick movements, muttering something under his breath.

The Bee chuckled, "Oh ho now, you wouldn't be trying a little magic, would you? Ha! It will do you no good. You see, I took the precaution, you might say, yes, of putting you back under the Counter-Spell as soon as Ozma returned you to your natural self. Humph, hmmm. We would not want any fresh outbreak of mischief now, would we?"

Realizing that the cats were becoming uneasy, Ozma decided it was time for her pronouncement. Standing on top of the parapet where all could see and hear, she stated clearly, "You have rebelled and rebellion must be punished. The Spelling Bee has removed the Counter-Spell from you, so you are no longer protected from our magic."

A palpable shiver could be seen to run through the assembly of felines. The Queen allowed it to run its course, letting them feel the fear. Then she resumed, "Although we could punish you in any way we might wish, we will be fair. We will not inflict pain upon you, but your punishment will fit your crimes.

"Hear now my verdict.

"First: I decree that through the magic they sought to avoid, the power of speech will be taken from all cats for the period of two weeks, beginning immediately after my decrees are completed. Let the cats realize how much is theirs simply because they live in the Land of Oz.

"Second: I decree that since the rebels were cruel to the people they conquered, during that same two week period, all cats will truly be treated as subordinate creatures, not with vengeance or cruelty, simply as inferiors. Let the cats realize how much equality they already had in Oz.

"Third: I decree that since there was merit in the claim that cats were neither considered nor represented in the laws of the land, henceforth, a cat chosen by his fellow cats shall be included among my councilors. It shall be his or her duty to see that cats are properly considered and shall be responsible both to you and to me. Let the cats and all others know that we are just in Oz.

"There are two more decrees to be made: one concerning the final disposition of Joom, and one to appoint your choice to the Council. You have time now, but not too much, to make that choice. May you act more wisely than you did when you followed Joom."

As Ozma stepped off the parapet, the cats stood still, numbed both by the sudden reversal of their fate and the justice of these decrees. Vengeance was not extracted upon them, yet they would be punished and fairly so. Soon however, a mumble was heard as one and then another called for the destruction of Joom. Not long before, these same voices had cried out for Ozma's abdication. Now they turned on their former leader, and it was he they would destroy; Ozma they would obey.

An ugly mood had begun, so, to prevent further trouble, Honey Cat and Alexander came to the parapet and took turns calling out, "Enough! The time has come for action. Let us be about the business of choosing our representative."

During the next half hour, that is just what they did. When they declared that they were ready, Sir Hokus stepped out of the palace, saying, "Anon shalt we hear thy choice, but for the nonce, Queen Ozma wilt conduct ye proper punishment of yon rascally knave, Joom." Then, stepping aside, he made room for Ozma.

She moved forward to stand upon the same grassy knoll where Joom, as a cat, had stood earlier in the day. Here she could see all the cats and they could see her and what she would do with Joom. To her left stood Glinda; on her right, the Spelling Bee. Glinda's Guards were quickly putting in place a triple strand of ropes around the base of the hill to keep all others at a distance.

Once they were in place, the Cowardly Lion and Sir Hokus, with his sword drawn as an added precaution, escorted the wicked magician through a gap in the ropes and in front of the young Princess. Raising her voice, she proclaimed, "Joom began this evil mission when he took over the body of Binkie and left that poor cat with no self. His friends have been wondering what has

# The Punishment of Joom

become of the real Binkie. We will begin the answer to that question by turning Joom back into his semi-cat form of Binkie."

Silently, all who were present stood captivated, watching the ritual of the Spelling Bee. His antennae and arms moved in rhythm with his words, cancelling the Counter-spell he had placed on the evil magician. Now, Ozma could once again work her magic upon him and by the time the Bee had finished, her hands were upon her Magic Belt. As the last words of the Dis-Spell died away, the man was gone, and in his place stood the semi-cat, Binkie-Joom.

Now Glinda stepped forward, and, spreading her arms wide, looking up to the sky, she began, in solemn voice, an incantation:

"Red power, good power, strong power,
Power of fairies and elves,
Power of all the elements be
Here in this mortal contained."

Not a sound was to be heard, not a murmur from the crowd, no rustling of leaves by playful wind. It was as though all the world waited. Then, the sound of a wind was heard, but quietly, as from afar, not loud, not wild. It came and went, and again, and again. The growing power in Glinda showed in the glow of her robes, upon her face and in her hands.

There was silence, silence as of the depths of time.

Quietly at first, and then with rising intensity, Glinda's

voice could be heard once more:

> "Dark is dark, and light is light.
> Here we have the two in one.
> Such conflict raves and cannot be.
> Now by all the powers of light,
> Out. Out, I demand of you.
> Out of him."

At the last she was shouting. Then, silence again. But, in the silence, the scraggly black cat flopped over on his side. Then he began to twitch and turn, to wiggle and jump. Suddenly he went high into the air, and disappeared. Even Glinda looked bewildered as she shook her head. No one moved. The Red Sorceress was saying slowly, "Something's gone wrong ... ," when there was a small flash and the cat came down, but now he was two! Side by side stood the cat, Binkie, and the other, the wicked magician, Joom.

Both of them looked confused by the sudden splitting. Even the magician looked around himself, dazed. He started to take a step and met the sharp sword and piercing eyes of Sir Hokus. Turning to retreat, he was almost engulfed by the wide mouth of the Cowardly Lion. Wisely, he stood still.

The cat had just crouched there. Now he shook himself, asking, "Wh-where am I? What's happened?" He paused. Then looking at the crowd of cats, he smiled and exclaimed, "I remember, I was drowning. And Merle was right. We've died and gone to heaven."

# The Punishment of Joom

"No, no," broke in Alexander from beyond the ropes, "not yet."

"You're right" replied the other, "Yes. I did get ashore with … . But where is Merle?"

"Who?"

"Merle. He was my friend."

"Merle Sprekless, you mean?" asked Alexander.

"Yes. Oh, that's right. This confounded man next to me did something with him, and I couldn't find him."

"Was Merle … "

"Wait!" cried Glinda. "Something is happening. I can feel the power. Immense pow …"

Her voice and the very scene were drowned out by a tremendous roar and flash of light. When people could see once more, there were not two separate beings standing before her, but three — the scraggly black cat, the wickedly ugly man, and a simple looking hobo.

Pandemonium broke loose. Every one was asking questions and moving through the broken ropes toward the trio. Honey Cat and Alexander were the first to reach Binkie. The Lion and Sir Hokus were now immediately before and behind Joom. Several of the other American cats were with the other man, meowing, "Merle, what are you doing here?"

Ozma raised her hand for silence and turned to Glinda.

The Red Sorceress announced, "Apparently Joom had more transformations up his sleeve than we had thought. That was why there was a delay in my transformation-breaking. It had to disentangle three beings instead of

227

just the two I had prepared for, and the extra power required was so great as to cause all that light and sound. How a third being got in there, I cannot imagine."

"I think that before I pronounce sentence on Joom," indicated Ozma, "he will tell us what happened."

In response, Joom stood firmly, scowling at her.

"Yes," nodded the Good Witch, "I believe he will. Golnora, will you bring me my White Pearl and my Red Pearl? Thank you. In the meantime, let us see if Binkie can help us."

Alexander, Honey Cat and Binkie had slipped off to the shadow of the wall where they were catching up on each other's adventures. However, they responded to Glinda's calling them, but Binkie could only tell her that Merle had disappeared after a night of nightmares and Joom had appeared that next morning.

This was a beginning, but Glinda and Ozma wanted to know much more. Soon, when Golnora returned with a large golden box, she opened the container for Glinda and there lay two brightly gleaming jewels. The Sorceress took them out and hung them around her neck.

Taking Joom by the arm, she said, "Look here. What do you see hanging around my neck?"

"A gold chain."

"And on it?"

"What looks like a white pearl and a red pearl."

"Look closely at them."

"Yes. That's still what they look like."

"Ah, you're quite right, but keep on looking. Intently. A moment longer." Then, after a pause, "Now what do

# The Punishment of Joom

you see?"

"Why there is just one pearl and it is pink."

"Very good! Now, tell me how you managed to get you and Binkie and Merle all into one being. And you jumped back and forth, only between Binkie and Joom."

"I'm not, ah, I …"

"That's all right. Take your time and speak clearly. You have just been the victim of a bit of good magic. Looking so intently at the two pearls made it impossible for you to give me anything but full and truthful answers, once you saw them as one pink one. Now, go ahead."

With a sigh of resignation, the evil magician said, "I … . It was very complicated Yookoohoo magic. The cave that Binkie and Merle found was mine. I had been magically transformed, but the presence of Merle made it possible for me to take over his body while he dreamed one night. That was relatively easy. The next step was more difficult. I didn't want to loose Merle, but I needed to be a cat, so a few days later, I turned Binkie into a jug. Then I could work at my own pace to make it possible for me to transform myself back and forth between Binkie and me. I could leave that pesky Merle out of it completely. Then I came to Oz, where, as a cat, I could convince the cats of Oz to rebel against that in … in … in … . I can't say it."

"Of course not. You were going to say something unkind about Ozma, and you cannot, for you have to be truthful."

"Anyway, I thought I had it all worked out," and his shoulders sagged as he finished, "now I'm all washed up."

# Toto and the Cats of Oz

"Yes, quite," responded Ozma. Then looking questioningly at Glinda, she said, "I believe we are now ready to finish my proclamations." With a nod from her friend, the little Queen, stepped in front of all, and speaking loudly once more, said, "Hear now my fourth decree: Since Joom, in his attempt to enslave Oz, both pretended to be a cat and tried to use the Counter-Spell, he shall finish his life as a cat under the protection of the Counter-Spell. Let the tools of his wickedness become the means of his punishment in Oz."

Before her last words were completed, Ozma's hands were already on her Magic Belt and instantly, Joom was once more a cat. But this was a cat such as no one had ever seen before. Like his human self, his face was deeply lined and his ears were big and round..

"You thought you would use cats to conquer us, now you shall finish your life as a cat." Then nodding to the Spelling Bee, she said, "And finish your life you will."

As the Spelling Bee quickly chanted the mysterious phrases of the Counter-Spell, Joom looked up at her, mystified, "What are you going to do to me now?"

"Nothing more," replied Ozma. "You are again under the Counter-Spell and no magic can turn you back to human form. No one can ever work magic upon you, and, as you already know, the power of this spell makes it impossible for you to perform any magic. However, what you might not have thought about before is the fact that even the deepest magic of Oz no longer has any effect upon you. In other words, you are no longer covered by the ancient spell of Lurline that long ago put

# The Punishment of Joom

an end to death and illness in Oz, and makes it possible for all its residents to stop aging whenever they wish. You will grow old and die. If you anger anyone too much, you can easily be killed. Finally, because of your unusual and inalterable appearance, all who meet you will remember that you once tried to enslave all Oz, and no one will trust you. You will be an outcast. You will be punished by the form and magic you tried to use against us. You can only hope that the people of Oz might be more merciful than were you."

Hearing the sentence passed upon him, the cat, Joom, cowered before Ozma. Then, realizing the truth of her words that all would distrust him, he could never again practice magic, and that his life was limited, he turned in fear, and fled into the woods where he would live out his short life, far from the haunts of men.

All, both cats and humans, had been enthralled by the events of Joom's punishment, but now it was necessary for Ozma to move on to the final proclamation. Turning to the assembled cats, she called out, "Hear now! The time has come for you to declare who your Representative will be. What is your choice?"

Just as the mob of cats had seemed to have a single voice when they chanted, "Abdicate. Abdicate," now they called out as one, "Honey Cat. Honey Cat."

As they called, Ozma turned to that beautiful cat, saying, "I had planned to send all the cats from America back to their own homes tomorrow evening. Are you willing to stay on alone?"

"If these marvelous new friends of mine want me, I

will stay to do their bidding."

At that, the nearby cats led a shout again of, "Honey Cat. Honey Cat," which was quickly taken up by the rest of them.

Holding up her hands for silence, the Queen declared, "So shall it be. My fifth and final decree is this: since you have chosen Honey Cat, he shall be your representative among my councilors. May he always and faithfully represent the cats of Oz.

"With these words, the magic charm is completed that removes the power of speech from all cats for two weeks."

Immediately, there was a chorus of meows as the cats tried to respond and found that true enough, their power of speech was gone. Then, chastened and quiet, they parted to return to their own homes.

One small group of cats remained behind. These were the cats from America. They had no homes in Oz, and no idea how to find their way back to Seattle. Understanding the plight of his friends, Alexander and Honey Cat rounded them up and brought them to where Ozma stood.

Here, with gentle words of reassurance, she welcomed them to join in the next day's celebration at Christmas Valley. "Tomorrow night you will go to sleep in Santa's Inn. The next morning you will wake up in your usual waterfront haunts in Seattle."

Then, calling the people to come close around her, Ozma said, "I have one more special decree to make, one which we did not discuss in Glinda's Council chamber.

# The Punishment of Joom

In the first place, all of you responded willingly to my call for help. Secondly, despite my law against it, in the past I have raised no objection to the innocent magic which most of you have performed. Thirdly, having asked for your help in this time of trouble, I can hardly require you to stop doing what, previously, I have privately allowed. Therefore, I decree that henceforth, for you, and for you only, the ban on working magic in Oz is lifted. As a reward for having helped, magic is now legal for you, but only helpful, innocent or entertaining magic. And be sure to heed the warning of the Spelling Bee, that your help be truly helpful. This entire trouble with the cats started when he *thought* he was being helpful to cats in distress. Let your powers be used wisely and safely. So be it."

There was much satisfied murmuring among the gathered friends. Each of the workers of magic, in one way or another expressed her or his thanks to Ozma for her generosity.

After all had been said that needed to be, and with dusk rapidly falling upon the land, Glinda stepped to the fore, saying, "You are all invited to come into the palace for a dinner of rejoicing."

As they went in, Toto fell in step beside Ozma, and, looking up at her said, "What about that Holder that was taking me up the mountain? Where was he taking me and why?"

"He is well known to me and to many Ozians. He will hold anything for anyone, irrespective of who they are. It is a matter of honor with him that he pays no attention to what a person wants him to hold, nor to his reason for wanting him to. He guarantees the safety and security of the thing held."

"Then I guess he failed with me, didn't he?"

"Yes. I believe you are a first. I have never heard of him failing before. But, you may have noticed Glinda's Swan Cart take off a few minutes ago. Glinda and I have sent Permina to tell him that he need not worry about that guarantee. His reputation has not been hurt."

# Chapter 24

# A Celebration in Christmas Valley

he next morning found everyone on the way to Christmas Valley. Using her Magic Belt, Ozma had both brought her Red Wagon back from where they had left it in the brushes when they fled the cats, and repaired it. Now she rode in it, leading the most fantastic of parades. Everyone had joined the march. Some had taken on special forms. Some flew and some rode, but all moved together. The Red Wagon was full. Glinda's Stork Cart had returned and was full. Above them flew several who had transformed themselves into eagles. The Cowardly Lion carried a full load on his back, all made light by the Spelling Bee's Lightness Spell. Besides that, one of that marvelous creature's Speed Spells helped to make a short trip out of what would have been a trip of several days.

Although joyous, the trip was uneventful. Arriving at the mountain pass leading into Christmas Valley, everyone was awed by the glorious sight spread out before them. To top it off, there, coming up the hill to meet them, was good old St. Nick, himself, who had returned the night before to prepare a celebration.

# Toto and the Cats of Oz

The dinner was scheduled for four PM, for it was a very grand one. There was salmon and turkey and goose and roast beef. There were sweet potatoes and white potatoes, each prepared in three different ways. All kinds of delectable vegetables were available. There was cranberry sauce, several kinds of gravy and even more kinds of chutney. All could be washed down with either red or green Christmas punch. Then came desert — an endless variety of pies, cookies, cakes and ice cream. Everyone was laughing and talking. Speeches were given. Old friendships were renewed and new ones were begun.

Finally, about six-thirty, Santa Claus rapped loudly on his glass of punch. The crowd quieted for about the tenth time that evening, and he announced, "What a wonderful company you have been this evening. If I do say so myself, I believe my elves have outdone themselves with the delightful repast they have provided us. But now, the time has come for outdoor sport. We have sleds and skis and skates, even a couple of toboggans, and all the outdoors awaits you. The ice pond is out back over to your right as you leave through that door." He motioned with his right hand. "The slopes for skis and sleds are to the left with plenty of each at the top. The toboggans I will bring out later. And snow? In endless quantity for whatever sport you wish. So now, it is all yours."

There was a grand cheer as chairs scraped, boots clattered and everyone got up and headed for the out-of-doors. People, animals and whatever lived and moved enjoyed themselves that night. Eventually, people began

# A Celebration in Christmas Valley

to tire and one by one, or two by two or several at a time, they began to seek their rooms for the night.

As the crowd grew smaller, Santa finally called out, "Many of us have already turned in for the night and I believe the time has come for the rest of us to follow suit. There were some complaints, a few who found it hard to quit, but most were ready and it did not take long to clear the slopes and the ice.

That night, sitting on the edge of her bed, Dorothy picked up her dog, and cuddling him close, she said, "Oh Toto! I am so happy that everything has finally turned out all right. I was so worried about you."

"Yup," replied her little dog, "but the credit goes to Alexander, there. Without him, no telling what might have happened."

The big cat responded in cat-like fashion by stretching and licking his paws.

"You are right," exclaimed Dorothy, "and when we awaken in the morning he will not even be with us anymore. Here kitty, kitty, kit ... Oh, excuse me. I mean, come on Alexander, you jump up here, too."

Stepping daintily and casually, the big gray-striped cat moved over to the bed and, with one indifferent leap, landed on Dorothy's lap, settling down there and crowding Toto off a little to the side. He looked at the dog, winked one eye at him, and began to purr with the pure contentment of a satisfied cat.

# Index and Identification

# Who's Who

**Alexander** – A big, tough cat from Seattle, half alley cat and half wildcat. Joom uses him as a cat to guard Toto, but he becomes disenchanted with Joom.

**Army of Oz** – See OMBY AMBY.

**Aunt Em** (Auntie Em) – Dorothy's aunt who originally lived in Kansas, but now lives in the Emerald City. From *The Wizard of Oz*.

**Baluol** – The head chef in Ozma's Palace. Alexander Volkov's Russian Oz books. (*a* as in act, *u* as in unit, *o* as in odd; Bal-u'ol)

**Betsy Bobbin** – A little girl from Oklahoma that was on an ocean trip when the ship blew up and she ended up on the shores of the Rose Kingdom, eventually making her way to Oz, where she has stayed. From *Tik-Tok of Oz*.

**Binkie** – A bedraggled black cat from the docks of Seattle that is taken over by the evil Joom.

**Bragwost** – Author of *History of Eastern Ozia,* where it is found that the wicked magician that turned Prince Bobo into a goat is named "Joom." (*Brag* like brag, *o* as in odd; Brag'wost)

**Bungle** – The Glass Cat that Dr. Pipt brought to life with his Powder of Life. From *The Patchwork Girl of Oz*.

# Toto and the Cats of Oz

**Button-Bright** – A young boy from Philadelphia who has been lost so often that he finally settled in Oz where, although he still gets lost, is always found. From *Sky Island*.

**Cap'n Bill** – A ship's captain who lost his leg and, land bound, became a companion for Trot, accompanying her to Oz. From *Sea Fairies*.

**Captain General** – See OMBY AMBY.

**Cowardly Lion** – One of Dorothy's earliest friends in Oz, the humbug Wizard gave him a potion to eliminate his cowardliness, but the image of it soon returned. That is he says he is afraid, but in a showdown, he is quite brave. From *The Wizard of Oz*.

**Dorothy** – Queen Ozma's closest friend, originally from Kansas. From *The Wizard of Oz*.

**Em** – See AUNT EM.

**Eureka** – The cat that Dorothy found in San Francisco and took with her on her third trip to Oz. Although originally white, the different colored suns of Mangaboo caused her to change colors, a trait that has stayed with her. Or was she originally from Oz and had that trait all along? From *Dorothy and the Wizard in Oz*.

**Gillikins** – The people who live in the north of Oz, Gilli-kinland. From *The Land of Oz*.

**Glass Cat** – See BUNGLE.

**Glinda** – The Good Witch of the South and ruler of the Quadlings. From *The Wizard of Oz*.

**Golnora** – One of Glinda's Girl Guards from the Gillikin Country. (*Gol* as in golly, *nora* as in Nora; Gol-nor'a)

**Henry** – See UNCLE HENRY.

240

# Who's Who

**Holder, The** – He runs an Ozian version of a public locker and guarantees to keep it safe.

**Hungry Tiger** – Although always hungry for a fat baby, his conscience will not let him eat one. In general, always hungry for anything. From *Ozma of Oz*.

**Jack Pumpkinhead** – A man that the young Ozma made out of a jack-o'lantern, sticks and old clothes, that Mombi brought to life, just to see if the Powder of Life worked. From *The Land of Oz*.

**Jellia Jamb** – Has two jobs. One is to be Ozma's personal maid. The other is that she is in charge of the Palace's household staff. (*Jell* like jell, *i* as in machine, *a* as in another; *Jamb* like jam; Jel'li-a Jamb)

**Joom** – The villain of the story, a wicked magician that takes over both the hobo Merle Sprekless and the cat Binkie. Eventually he tries to take over Oz.

**Jule Nissen** – The Danish Christmas elf who keeps the household running smoothly all year but who eats only on Christmas Eve, and that, because food is given to him by the children, and all childlike celebrators. (*Jule* like Yule; *i* as in machine, *e* as in end; Jule Nis'sen)

**King of Ev** – This is the one that had ruled Ev before Ozma went to Ev to save his family. From *Ozma of Oz*.

**Merle Sprekless** – The vagrant that hung around the Seattle docks and whose personality was ultimately taken over by Mooj. (*Merle* like Merle; *e* as in end, *less* like less; Merle' Sprek'less)

**Mombi** – Once the Wicked Witch of the North, after she was deposed, she still held Ozma captive, relearned magic and was a trouble maker. From *The Land of Oz*.

241

**Munchkins** - The people who live in the east of Oz, Munchkinland. From *The Wizard of Oz.*

**Omby Amby** - This is the Soldier with Green Whiskers that met Dorothy and her friends when they first came to Oz. Later, Ozma promoted him from Private to Captain General. Since she then did away with all the rest of the army, he is also known as the Army of Oz. From *The Wizard of Oz* and *Ozma of Oz.*

**Ozians** - Inhabitants of Oz.

**Ozma** - Queen of Oz, frequently referred to as a princess. From *The Land of Oz.*

**Patchwork Girl** - See SCRAPS.

**Permina** (*Perm* like perm, *i* as in machine, *a* as in another; Per-mi'na) - One of Glinda's Girl Guards.

**Pipt, Dr.** - Also known as The Crooked Magician, not because he was dishonest, but because he became so misshapen through mnay years of stirring the Powder of Life. From *The Patchwork Girl of Oz.*

**Quadlings** - The people who live in the south of Oz, Quadlingland. From *The Wizard of Oz.*

**Sawhorse** - See WOODEN SAWHORSE.

**Scarecrow** - Dorothy's first friend in Oz. From *The Wizard of Oz.*

**Scraps** - A patchwork doll made by Margolotte Pipt and brought to life by Dr. Pipt. From *the Patchwork Girl of Oz.*

**Shaggy Man** - A hobo in America, he has become a loyal friend and a frequent explorer in Oz. From *The Road to Oz.*

**Sir Hokus of Pokes** - A knight of the Medieval type that is frequently in the Emerald City. From *The Cowardly Lion of Oz.*

# Who's Who

**Smith and Tinker** – A famous partnership of engineers that invented a number of mechanical marvels, including Tik-Tok (q.v.). From *Ozma of Oz*.

**Soldier with Green Whiskers** – See OMBY AMBY.

**Teriane** – Captain of Glinda's Girl Guards. (*Teri* like Terry, *ane* as in bane; Ter-i-ane')

**Tik-Tok** – The mechanical man, invented by Smith and Tinker, but rescued by Dorothy when she was first in Ev. From *Ozma of Oz*.

**Tin Woodman** – One of Dorothy's earliest friends in Oz. From *The Wizard of Oz*.

**Tinker** – See SMITH AND TINKER.

**Toto** – Dorothy's dog and constant companion. From *The Wizard of Oz*.

**Trot** – A little girl that came to Oz from near San Diego, California, and stayed. From *Sea Fairies*.

**Uncle Henry** – Dorothy's uncle, originally from Kansas, but now living in the Emerald City. From *The Wizard of Oz*.

**Winkies** – The people who live in the west of Oz, Winkieland. From *The Wizard of Oz*.

**Wizard of Oz** – Originally, he came to Oz in a balloon and ruled in the Emerald City for many years, before Dorothy and her friends discovered him to be a humbug. He left Oz then, but came back in a few years, and became a real wizard, trained by Glinda. From *The Wizard of Oz*.

**Wooden Sawhorse** – A carpenter's sawhorse that Ozma brought to life when she first fled from the Wicked Witch, Mombi. From *The Land of Oz*.

**Woozy** – A very leathery creature made entirely from rectangular parts. From *The Patchwork Girl of Oz*.

# Where's Where

**Ballroom** – The Ballroom of the Palace in the Emerald City.

**County Home** – The home for indigent old folks in Kansas that Aunt Em and Uncle Henry would have had to go to, when they could not pay back their farm loan. From *The Emerald City of Oz*.

**Dining Room** – In the Palace, this room is sometimes referred to as the Great Dining Room, in contrast to the smaller dining room. From.

**Emerald City** – Capital of Oz and home of Ozma and many of the main characters in the Oz books. From *The Wizard of Oz*.

**Great Garden** – A beautifully designed and very large garden outside Ozma's apartments.

**Great Gates of the Garden** – The formal entrance to the Great Garden.

**Hammerhead Mountains** – Mountains a little north of Glinda's Palace that are home to a race of armless people with stretchable necks that allow their heads to be used as battering rams. From *The Wizard of Oz*.

**Kansas** – Dorothy's original home. From *The Wizard of Oz*.

**Land of Oz** – Sometimes Oz is referred to as "The Land of Oz."

**Munchkin Mountains** – A range of mountains in Munckinland.

**Munchkin River** – A river forming part of the boundary between Munchkinland and the Emerald City area and flowing through most of the north of Munchkinland. From *The Wizard of Oz*.

**Nonestic Ocean** – The ocean that surrounds the continent Oz is on. From *Pirates in Oz*.

**Pokes** – A country where everyone is practically asleep all the time. From *The Cowardly Lion of Oz*.

**Quadling Country** – The southern part of Oz. From *The Wizard of Oz*.

**Throne Room** – The room where, originally, the Wizard gave audience to Dorothy and her friends. It is now Ozma's Throne Room and is located next to the Ballroom on the main floor of the Palace in the Emerald City.

**Wizard's Workshop** – It is located high in a tower of the Palace. From *The Scalawagons of Oz*.

# What's What

**Great Book of Records** – This possession of Glinda's records everything as it happens, but very briefly. From *The Emerald City of Oz*.

**Magic Belt** – Originally owned by the wicked Nome King, Dorothy took it from him when she helped Ozma rescue the Royal Family of Ev. It can be used for transformations and transportation as well as doing other kinds of magic. From *Ozma of Oz*.

**Magic Picture** – A picture Ozma has that will show you any place or person you wish to see. From *Ozma of Oz*.

**Magic Record Book** – See GREAT BOOK OF RECORDS.

**Peerless Expanding Enhancing Compound** – A compound made by Dr. Pipt that causes things to grow much bigger than normal.

**Powder of Life** – Invented by Dr. Nikidik, but also used by Dr. Pipt. The latter used it to bring to life, among others, Bungle, the Glass Cat and the Patchwork Girl. From *The Patchwork Girl of Oz*.

**Queen's Council** – The group of Ozian luminaries that serve as advisors to Ozma.

**Red Wagon** – The stout, good sized wagon that the Sawhorse pulls. From *The Land of Oz*.

# OZ

If you have enjoyed this book, you might be interested in the International Wizard of Oz Club. Not only does it publish, three times a year, a magazine with much valuable information and opinion about Oz and things related to it, but it also arranges for regional meetings of people interested in Oz and tells you about other Oz events going on in the world.

Contact:
The International Wizard of Oz Club,
P. O. Box 2657,
Alameda CA,
94501, USA,
or www.ozclub.org

***What is an Oz book?*** A few people declare that only *The Wizard of Oz* is eligible. A few more limit them to the books by L. Frank Baum. Most people accept the Famous Forty, that is the 39 Oz books published by Reilly & Britton and its successor, Reilly and Lee, plus *The Wizard of Oz*. Many, including this author, accept three more categories: the Borderland of Oz books (Baum's other fairy tales that are brought into the Oz series by characters from those books appearing in the Famous Forty); any other Oz book written by the authors of the Famous Forty; and any published by the International Wizard of Oz Club. In the list below, this author adds to those  any other Oz books written in the spirit of the Baum-Thompson books. Of course that is a highly subjective standard of judgment, but in the following list, that means the seven Shanower books, and some by Gjovaag-Carlson, Hess and Eichorn. Other people would include any book that has the word Oz in the title, extending the list to hundreds.

Most Oz books and Borderland of Oz books are available, used and sometimes new, from amazon.com or Books of Wonder, 16 W. 18th Street, New York, NY 10011 - www.booksofwonder.com. Several, as noted, are more easily available from Hungry Tiger Press, 5995 Dandridge Lane, Suite 121, San Diego CA 92115, www.hungrytigerpress.com, or International Wizard of Oz Club, P.O. Box 26249, San Francisco CA 9426-6249, www.ozclub.org [IWOC]

# The Oz Books

**By L. Frank Baum**

*The Wizard of Oz*
*The Magical Monarch of Mo*
*Dot and Tot of Merryland*
*The Life and Adventures of
    Santa Claus*
*The Enchanted Island of Yew*
*The Land of Oz*
*Queen Zixi of Oz*
*John Dough and the Cherub*
*Ozma of Oz*
*Dorothy and the Wizard of Oz*
*The Road to Oz*

*The Emerald City of Oz*
*Sea Fairies*
*Sky Island*
*The Patchwork Girl of Oz*
*Tik-Tok of Oz*
*The Scarecrow of Oz*
*Rinkitink in Oz*
*The Lost Princess of Oz*
*The Tin Woodman of Oz*
*The Magic of Oz*
*Glinda of Oz*

**By Ruth Plumly Thompson**

*The Royal Book of Oz*
*Kabumpo in Oz*
*The Cowardly Lion of Oz*
*Grampa in Oz*
*The Lost King of Oz*
*The Hungry Tiger of Oz*
*The Gnome King of Oz*
*The Giant Horse of Oz*
*Jack Pumpkinhead of Oz*
*The Yellow Knight of Oz*

*Pirates in Oz*
*The Purple Prince of Oz*
*Ojo in Oz*
*Speedy in Oz*
*The Wishing Horse of Oz*
*Captain Salt in Oz*
*Handy Mandy in Oz*
*The Silver Princess in Oz*
*Ozoplaning with the Wizard
    in Oz*

**By John R. Neill**

*The Wonder City of Oz*
*The Scalawagons of Oz*
*Lucky Bucky in Oz*

By Jack Snow
*The Magical Mimics in Oz*
*The Shaggy Man of Oz*

By Rachel Cosgrove Payes
*The Hidden Valley of Oz*

By Eloise Jarvis McGraw &
   Lauren McGraw Wagner
*Merry Go Round in Oz*

By Ruth Plumly Thompson
*Yankee in Oz*
*The Enchanted Island of Oz*

By Eloise Jarvis McGraw &
   Lauren McGraw Wagner
*The Forbidden Fountain of Oz*

By Dick Martin
*The Ozmapolitan of Oz*

By Eric Shanower (graphic
   novels)
*The Enchanted Apples of Oz*
   [HTP]
*The Secret Island of Oz* [HTP]
*The Ice King of Oz* [HTP]
*The Forgotten Forest of Oz*
   [HTP]
*The Blue Witch of Oz* [HTP]

By Rachel Gosgrove Payes
*The Wicked Witch of Oz*
   [IWOC]

By Eric Shanower
*The Giant Garden of Oz*

By Eric Gjovaag & Karyl
   Carlson
*Queen Ann of Oz*

By John R. Neill
*The Runaway in Oz*

By Robin Hess
*Christmas in Oz*
*Toto and the Cats of Oz*

By Virginia Wickwar
*The Hidden Prince of Oz*
   [IWOC]

By Eloise Jarvis McGraw
*The Rundelstone of Oz* [HTP]

By Eric Shanower
*The Salt Sorcerer of Oz* [HTP]

By Edward Eichorn
*The Living House of Oz* [HTP]

By Virginia Wickwar
*Toto of Oz* [IWOC]

Made in the USA
Charleston, SC
15 December 2014